Left for Death

By

Joseph D'Aquisto

Chapter 1

July 19, 2005

    I opened the door to Leo Johnson's apartment. His employer had filed a police report that morning stating that Johnson had not been to work in three days. Nobody had heard from him, he had not called in sick, and he had no direct family who had been in contact with him recently. No wife or kids. I received the call at approximately 9:30 a.m. I arrived at Johnson's apartment building at 10:15 a.m. The secretary in the main office directed me to his apartment. When I banged loudly on the door, there was no answer. I turned the door handle. It was locked. I went to the apartment office and had the secretary unlock the door for me. I entered the apartment. It was a decent-sized place, not luxurious but roomy. White walls, light green carpet. The kitchen was located immediately to my right. I looked toward the living area and saw a tan fabric couch with a TV facing directly across from it on a small entertainment stand against the wall. Everything was perfectly neat. No signs of struggle or forced entry. I examined the area. Nothing.

    As I walked further down the hallway, approaching the back of the apartment I saw a door that was most likely the bathroom. It was closed. I suddenly had a terrible feeling in my gut; I smelled a strong odor coming from the other side. I took a deep breath. I was going to open the door fast. Doing it slowly is much worse because all it does is delay the suspense. Better to get it over with. I turned the handle and the door flew open. The stench thickened. I saw a man's body lying in the bathtub, dried blood stains on the tiles. The lights were still on.

I leaned over the body to get a closer look and saw a bullet hole in his forehead. Aw, Christ. I was sure it was the body of Leo Johnson, although I would have to confirm that later after I got a forensics team down to identify him.

I had seen many dead bodies in my career as a detective, but that didn't mean I had learned to like it. I quickly put on latex gloves before covering my mouth and nose with one hand so that I wouldn't vomit.

I touched his hand. It felt cool, but his skin still looked fresh and didn't show much decomposition. After death, body temperature declines progressively until it reaches the temperature of its surroundings. Usually, the process takes between eight and twelve hours on the skin, but the center of the body takes about three times as long. Judging from this, I estimated that he had been dead for approximately twenty-four to forty-eight hours, but I wasn't positive. I'd leave the final analysis to the forensics experts.

I came out of the bathroom and slammed the door shut, wanting to escape the stench. I used my cell phone to dial the forensics team at headquarters.

"Parker speaking," the voice answered. Clay Parker was one of the head crime lab analysts on the forensics team.

"Yeah, Parker, this is Detective Sandes. I got a dead body up here. Maybe a homicide." I told him the details and gave him the address.

"I'll be there with a team right away."

The examination team arrived fifteen minutes later. They immediately photographed the entire scene before touching anything else. They took blood samples and searched for other traces of evidence on the body. Meanwhile, I examined the rest of the apartment. I walked into the bedroom, and the first thing I saw was a small photograph on the edge of his bed. The picture showed a little blond-haired, blue-eyed girl. She looked to be no more than ten. That was interesting since Johnson had no immediate family. It couldn't be his kid. I took a photo of the picture with my phone and alerted one of the forensic techs to examine it. I found a ring of keys on his kitchen table and picked them up. Nothing looked unusual to me. The bed was made and tidy. Johnson had a bookshelf with several books and videos.

I spent a couple of hours searching through the apartment, and I spoke with neighbors. None of them had heard a gunshot. So far, I didn't have any leads to go on. By the time I was done searching I had a pounding headache and was ready to leave. I didn't think I needed to look at anything else. I checked with the rest of the examination team to see if they had found anything significant. I looked over and spotted a technician leaning over the body taking tissue samples.

"So, what do you think?" I asked the tech, a young male in his late twenties.

"Well, not much yet, besides the obvious. Gunshot wound. Bullet hole right in the middle of his forehead."

I'll follow up with them later for more information when the autopsy is complete. I went out into the hallway and immediately spotted Parker. Parker, a brown-haired man of medium height and build. I walked over to him, "If your team happens to find anyone else's prints or signs of evidence, let me know."

"Yes, of course, Detective."

I decided to go home to think more about this case. There was not much else I could do there. It was 1:00 in the afternoon. I had a headache. I pulled a packet of Tylenol from my coat pocket. I had been working a lot, as usual, putting in almost seventy-five hours between the office and home, and hadn't slept much lately. I arrived at my apartment approximately twenty minutes later. I entered, removing both my madras hat and trench coat, and placing them on the hook on the back of the door. I removed my holster, which held my Smith and Wesson .38 automatic pistol. I went into the bathroom and took a look at myself in the mirror. My eyes had big bags underneath them. My hair looked a mess. I'm completely bald on top, so to compensate for it, I grow it long on the right side and comb it over the top of my head to the left side. Whenever I took off my hat, all my hair flipped over so that it was completely hanging off the side, making me look like some sort of madman. People have been telling me for years now to clip it and accept that I am bald, but I just don't want to do it.

I turned on the faucet and splashed some water on my face. God, I felt so damn tired. I was starting to feel my age kick in. At 65 years old, I knew my youth was long gone, but the job had been taking more out of me than ever. My body wasn't what it used to be either. I'm five foot ten inches tall and weigh 200. Not a terrible weight. Sure, I was still in pretty decent physical shape. My shoulders and biceps were still pretty muscular, but my stomach has gotten considerably larger during the last several years, acquiring an alarming amount of flab. I remembered how I had barely weighed 160 when I was thirty. Guess you can't fight against time. I looked at myself a moment longer before I went back into the kitchen and brewed a pot of coffee.

I sat down on my couch and flipped through a *Far Side* book. I've always thought Gary Larson's comics were hilarious. He has a unique sense of humor. Reading these books helps me get my mind off my job when I need to relax. *The Far Side Gallery 3* was dedicated to my brother, Billy, who was once friends with Gary. After a few minutes of reading, I looked up to reflect on my life.

I was divorced—for the second time. Have been for almost 15 years. I once had a family, but they're all out of my life now. It has been hard the past several years. I divorced my second wife because I could not deal with all the drama that had occurred shortly before our breakup. She'd started to lose her sanity. I felt deceived because she had lied about so many things during our marriage. We had numerous arguments and plenty of distress in those years, but the worst of it was the effect on my daughter. I felt sad for her most of all.

Mallory. I had not seen her in years. Mallory is my daughter from my first marriage to Joan, which was doomed from the beginning. Having Mallory was the best thing about it. I miss her every day. I want to talk to her, but she disappeared a long time ago. She did this on her own, but I knew deep inside that I was the one who had pushed her away. My second ex-wife Samantha, and Mallory had never gotten along. When Samantha and I were married, the relationship between the three of us had never gone well. It was like they competed for my attention.

I remembered the day Samantha came to me with an ultimatum. She told me that she wanted Mallory out of the house and out of our life. Mallory was in her early twenties at the time, living and attending college in Massachusetts, Boston University. She had traveled back home with a college friend, Nikki, to stay for a week while they were both on a school break. Samantha and Mallory argued the previous night concerning Mallory's friend. Mallory told us that she and Nikki were dating.

Samantha went ballistic, screaming at her, "I don't want some damn lesbians staying in our house! Get the hell out!" I tried unsuccessfully to calm Samantha down, to rationalize with her. Later, she approached me.

"It's either me or her. You choose."

I chose Samantha.

I talked to Mallory a few times over the phone shortly after that. She said she wasn't gay, just going through a "phase." She eventually met a guy she liked, who became her boyfriend. It didn't matter to me whether she was gay or not, I still loved her and I always will. I told this to Samantha, but she'd made up her mind. She didn't want to talk to Mallory. She wanted her out of our life.

"I'm sorry, Mallory," I blurted aloud. I did not need to think about this right now. I had enough on my mind. I grabbed the remote control and switched on the TV to watch the news. As I sat down on the couch, I felt my exhaustion take over. I closed my eyes and fell into a deep sleep.

At 6:15 p.m., I awoke to my phone ringing. I must have dozed off before I had a chance to even drink my coffee. The television was still on. I quickly turned it off.

"Hello?" I answered.

"John, it's Larry. How you doing, ol' man?" Larry Wegmueller was the Chief of Police, my direct supervisor.

"Doing fine, Larry. Taking a nap." I wondered groggily if I should admit that to my boss.

"I understand you caught a big one this morning."

"Yeah. I haven't got too much info yet. Just barely scratching the surface."

"Look, I know you've caught more than your share of cases lately. Let me know if you need any help. You get burned out on this one, I could find someone else to work it if you want."

"Relax, Larry. I'm fine. I'll call you if I need anything, I promise."

"All right. Talk to you later."

"Bye."

Larry worries too damn much.

I reheated the coffee, filled my mug, and walked over to the computer in the study. I pulled out my phone and looked at the picture of the girl I'd found at Johnson's apartment. I sat down at my computer and started doing some online digging. After several hours of mining through missing person reports, I came across a face that resembled the girl in the photo. K.C. Wingate. K.C. was eleven when she had been reported missing almost a month earlier. She had last been seen at school in her hometown of Clearview, located in the Seattle area—Snohomish County, not too far from the city. I had not heard of the case previously. It was out of my jurisdiction.

Was this child a victim of Johnson's killer as well? How were the two linked? I decided to investigate further and see what the Snohomish County Police found when they investigated. I searched through the online police reports but nothing was outstanding. Law enforcement had found no known links to her whereabouts. All the reports said that the last people to see the little girl were her school teachers. I made some notes from the reports and glanced at the clock. It was 11:45 p.m. I went to bed and awoke the next day at 6:00 a.m.

July 20

I made myself two cups of black coffee and watched the news for about an hour. I finally grabbed my trench and hat and got into my Honda Accord. One of these days I'm going to get a Corvette. I'd been telling myself that for years. I had owned a Corvette at one time in the sixties. Maybe one day I'd be rolling in the dough and be able to get another one. Oh, well.

I headed toward Clearview. I ran into some traffic and it took me a little over an hour. I felt that I was jumping the gun as far as heading straight to K.C.'s parents' house. It probably would have been better to call first, but I decided to take a more direct approach. It didn't look as if much progress had been made on the case.

I arrived and parked right across from the house, which happened to be in front of a neighborhood playground the size of a soccer field. The playground consisted of monkey bars, a few swing sets, and a slide. I looked around the neighborhood. It seemed like a nice, middle-class suburban area. I spotted two cars in the driveway and there were lights on inside, so I presumed everyone was at home.

I rang the doorbell. The door was answered by a tall, slender woman with dirty blond hair who appeared to be in her late thirties or early forties.

"Can I help you?"

"Yes, ma'am. Are you Mrs. Wingate?"

"Yes, I am. How can I help you?" she said, with a concerned look on her face.

"Mrs. Wingate, I am Detective Sandes with the Seattle Police Department. I am here in regards to your daughter, K.C. Is it okay if I ask you a few questions?"

Her expression changed quickly. "Have you found anything? I mean, did you find who took her?"

"Well—" I started but was quickly interrupted.

"Honey, who's at the door?" The voice belonged to a stocky man with light brown hair who looked slightly older than Mrs. Wingate.

"Hello, who are you?" he asked, appearing in the doorway.

"You're Mr. Wingate?"

"Yes, sir. Who are you? What's this about?"

Deciding to stretch the truth a bit, I replied, "I'm Detective Sandes. As I was telling your wife, Mr. Wingate, your daughter's case was transferred over to our district in the city, and, although we haven't found anything new, I just wanted to go back over the facts and make sure the reports that were submitted through the Clearview Police Station matched up to the information that I have. I'm sorry I came without calling, but I happened to be in the area. I hope I didn't disturb you."

The parents nodded and agreed to answer my questions.

"Did you have any relatives she stayed with occasionally?"

"No. I mean, we sometimes had a babysitter, Rosalyn, over to watch her when we went out to dinner. But Rosalyn always watched K.C. at our house," Mrs. Wingate replied while Mr. Wingate nodded.

"How long would Rosalyn typically watch her?"

"Never for more than just a few hours, maybe four at the most," Mr. Wingate said.

"There was no one else she may have stayed with? No friends or other relatives nearby in the Seattle area?"

"No. We have no other relatives nearby. It's been a while since she's stayed overnight at anyone's house. We usually have her friends stay over here. We have a pool out in the backyard that we installed several years ago, a foosball table downstairs, and the playground right across the street there." Mrs. Wingate pointed behind me. "Our house has become a popular place for slumber parties," she said.

The more she talked, the more nervous she seemed to be. I could see her hands were shaking. I'm sure the fact that we were using her daughter's name in the past tense rattled her.

"Do either of you know a Leo Johnson?" I asked. I pulled out my phone and showed them a photograph of him.

"No, why? Who is this person?" Mr. Wingate said as he studied the picture.

I didn't want him to suspect anything. "Not sure yet. A possible lead, maybe."

"No, I've never seen or talked with him. Do you think he took our little girl?" Mrs. Wingate said, staring fearfully at the photo.

I quickly put my phone back in my pocket. "Don't worry about this. I'm not positive of this man's involvement. Once again, I'm sorry. This case has been shared between different districts. All the police units in the area are cooperating to try and get your daughter back. I want to thank you both for your time and cooperation. I just wanted to assure you that we were still working on it. You can call me anytime you like. And if I hear anything, you two will be the first to know about it. I promise." I gave them my contact info as I left.

I knew that part of what I'd just said was bullshit, but I did not want to alarm K.C.'s parents with the news that I had just found their daughter's photo on the bed in some strange man's apartment. There was no need to say anything else until I was able to get more facts.

"Thank you, Detective," Mrs. Wingate said sadly, starting to cry.

"Honey, it's all right. They'll find her," Mr. Wingate said. He put his arm around her, trying to comfort her.

"Good night," I said giving a warm smile, trying my best to project confidence I did not feel.

I headed back to my car and drove off.

Chapter 2

July 21

At 6:00 a.m. sharp I awoke. I brewed a pot of coffee and took a shower. When I finished, I took another look at the photo of K.C. on my phone. The photo had been taken outdoors. I could make out some trees and a building or two in the frame. I'll see if I can have the original photo analyzed and zoom in on the background to get a better idea of where it may have been taken. I also planned to go back to Johnson's apartment and do another search just in case I had overlooked something.

    When I arrived back at Johnson's apartment, the body had been removed and the bloodstains were gone. Crime scene tape stretched over the apartment door. I checked the kitchen cabinets, fridge, under the sofa, and everywhere else I'd been, but saw nothing out of the ordinary. I went back into Johnson's bedroom and looked at his bookshelf. An avid reader, he had numerous books, and movies as well. The books were mixed fiction and nonfiction works by various authors, ranging from outdoor subjects such as *Nature Noir: A Park Ranger's Patrol in the Sierra* and *Frommer's Vancouver and Victoria 2005* to automobile volumes like *Porsche: The Road from Zuffenhausen*.

    I was about to leave the bedroom when I noticed something that seemed rather odd. Each book and videotape were covered in dust, except for one, *Conceptual Physics* by Paul G. Hewitt. A physics book did not seem to fit with the rest of his collection. Johnson had been a construction worker and for some reason, this one seemed off to me. I picked it up and flipped through it, I could tell it had been used recently. I continued to page through it. A small piece of paper fell out, almost like a homemade bookmark, cut from some sort of thick paper with a Celtic pattern drawn around the edges. Printed in the center were four sets of Roman numerals spaced evenly:

XXX XX XVIII XV

I decided to bring the physics book to the police station to have it checked for prints. Johnson had a small table next to his bed with a bundle of receipts on it. I had glanced at these yesterday as well. I flipped through them again. A few were fast-food purchases—McDonald's, Wendy's, Burger King. Some were for cash, while others were paid with a credit card. One of the charges was from an adult video store named Erotica Fliks and one from a U-Store-It Express. I grabbed them. After I was done, I headed back to my office downtown.

I parked my car and headed to see Parker at the crime lab.

I came through the front entrance, walking toward the back hallway where the main lab area was. When I entered, I saw a young technician, probably in his twenties. He was standing at a table, pouring some chemicals from a test tube into a graduated cylinder. I walked over to him.

"Excuse me, have you seen Parker?"

"I'm not sure where he is. He should be around the building somewhere."

"I believe this item may have been overlooked earlier during an investigation he was helping me with. Could you please give it to him? Have him check it for prints and examine it for DNA," I said to the technician.

"Sure thing, Detective."

The technician took the bag and carefully put it in a small metal box toward the back of the room.

As I walked back to my office building, my cell phone rang.

"Sandes speaking."

"John, it's me, Larry. What do you say to getting together with me and the boys for poker night down at Jimmy's?" Jimmy's was a popular sports restaurant downtown, where Larry, along with a couple of the detectives and some various businessmen from the Seattle area, met occasionally to play cards. They had a special table in the back reserved for Larry and his crew, which I commonly referred to as the "mafia booth."

It was the biggest table and was out of sight to most of the patrons in the restaurant, a concession to Larry's position in the city. He was a powerful man in Seattle. He had been police chief for the last 20 years and was highly commended when he took over the position and increased the department funds for equipment. The Seattle Police were known for having many of the newest and most innovative high-dollar forensic tools available. Our crime lab was ranked in the top five in the nation. Larry knew how to use his connections and influence. A man with his reputation was given certain considerations. I didn't mind playing poker, but I felt strange hanging out with those guys at that place. It made me feel like I was in some sort of gangster club, which isn't my style.

"No, but thanks. I think I'm going to bed a little early tonight." I wasn't in the mood for games.

"Aw, c'mon, John. It'll help you get your mind off things. You know it's always a great party when the Big Ox is around," Larry said with a hearty laugh. Larry still held the old nickname with honor, attained during his wrestling days back in college when he was also an avid weightlifter. He had earned that nickname for a reason. Although he was much older now, he was still built like an ox, and I certainly did not envy anyone who ended up in a physical altercation with him.

"No. Not tonight, Larry. Sorry," I said again.

"Suit yourself, ol' man. Just wanted to let you know the invitation is open. Drop by if you change your mind."

"Okay, Larry. Thanks." I ended the call. I hate it when Larry refers to me as "ol' man." It makes me feel exactly that: an old, vulnerable, weak man. I know I'm 65 and my mandatory retirement date is approaching later this year. There aren't too many people my age in the field. I'm the oldest detective on the Seattle police, but I'm not ready to hang it up just yet.

Besides, even though I was living comfortably now, I didn't have much of a retirement fund. I'd made some bad financial decisions in the past, which I was paying for now. I also mail out a check to Samantha every month. The two of us had decided not to use lawyers for any financial settlements and had agreed on an amount, even though what she got was more than she possibly needed. She was doing fine making a living as a con artist, as she had done for the last several years. Anyway, that was another story and I didn't want to think about her right now. I had agreed to the settlement because I felt it was the right thing to do. Larry, on the other hand, was in his early fifties, and as the chief of police he brought in well over a six-figure salary. He made more than your average chief, but that was because he was so good at it. Sometimes I envied him. He seemed to have his whole life in order. He was also divorced, but I hardly ever heard him talk about it.

    I approached my office building. I slipped through the front doors just as they closed behind a fairly tall man wearing a cowboy hat. Once inside, I passed all the clerks and receptionists with my head down and headed straight for my desk. I didn't want to be disturbed. One of the clerks, Penny, whose desk was right next to mine, would sometimes yak on the phone about her love problems. All I could do was hope things were going well for her today because frankly, I didn't want to hear it.

    I copied onto my computer all the images that had been taken at Johnson's apartment during the initial investigation. As I was looking through them, I came across one showing the bookshelf. Zooming in on the image, I got a more detailed look. There were numerous books about travel, and they were all related to Canada, most of them about Vancouver in particular. I pulled out the receipts I'd found earlier and flipped through them again. I noticed that the U-Store-It Express receipt had a Vancouver address on it. Now I was curious. What kind of connections did Johnson have in Vancouver? I was very interested to get up there and poke around. I thought about Johnson's murder and the fact that he was involved with some little girl and kept receipts from a porn store. That was a bad combination and I had a peculiar feeling this case was about to get ugly.

Chapter 3

For the next several hours I sat at my desk reviewing my notes and evidence. Parker called to inform me that his team had analyzed all the evidence. During the autopsy, the medical examiner had determined that the bullet that killed Johnson came from a .45 ACP handgun. They had found fragments of blond hairs on the victim's body. Johnson had dark brown hair, so they were not his. My mind went back to young K.C.

I remembered a young girl by the name of Katherine Mears who had been held hostage by two men underneath a garage. This occurred when I lived in New York, long before I ever became a detective, and within only an hour's distance from my house. The culprits were caught almost two months later. Under a garage! Jesus. What if K.C. were in a similar situation?

Glancing at my watch, I saw that it was almost 6:00 p.m. and decided to pay a little visit to Erotica Fliks to see if I could find out any information on Johnson. I looked up the address and found that it was roughly a twenty-minute drive away. Not too far.

I walked to the front entrance of my building. As soon as I opened the door, I saw that the sky was dark and cloudy, with rain pouring even though it had been clear just hours before. You gotta love the Pacific Northwest.

"Okay, this is going to take a little longer than I anticipated," I said aloud. I went back to my office to grab my coat and hat, got into my car, and headed off.

When I arrived in the area, I did not see the place immediately but parked anyway. I knew that I was on the right street, West Dravus in Magnolia, a town within the western part of Seattle, north of Elliott Bay and south of Shilshole Bay. Walking down the street, I searched for number 983. I knew I was close as I passed 969, a small convenience store on the left that was empty except for a lonely clerk standing outside the door smoking a cigarette. The area wasn't necessarily a bad one but seemed a bit shady. This part of town felt practically deserted. As I kept walking, I passed by number 985, a small house/apartment, and immediately came upon another building, 987. I couldn't have passed it. I turned back around, contemplating where to go.

I saw that there was a very narrow cobblestone alley between 985 and 981. What could be back there? It was extremely dark, but I thought I could see a faint light coming from a distance.

"This is odd," I said aloud.

As I slipped through the entrance to the alley, I saw that the very beginning of it was almost too narrow to fit. I had to step sideways to get through. Once I had gotten about ten feet through, the alley widened. As I walked down the corridor, I could see that it wrapped around another corner and that the light was getting brighter. When I finally got around the side, a door marked 983 appeared, though the 8 was hardly visible because the paint was worn. A small set of steps led to a doorway with a faint outdoor light directly above. It looked like somebody's house.

"This can't be the only way in here," I said to myself.

There was no doorbell, so I knocked and waited a moment. When there was no answer, I turned the door handle and found that it was unlocked. When I got inside, I saw an empty room with another door. A large sign on the door read:

PLEASE KNOCK TO ENTER

That was it. This couldn't be the right place. There was no business name or hours of operation. Nothing. I paused for a moment, listening as I held my ear to the door. I heard people talking. I knocked loudly. After a moment, a small horizontal slot in the door slid open to reveal two mean, shady-looking eyes.

"Who is it?" the voice said sternly.

"Yes, is this Erotica Fliks?" I asked.

"Do you have a club ID card?" the voice asked back.

"No, sir, but I would like to sign up for one."

"This is a private business facility, members only. You can't just walk in. Get the fuck outta here!"

Just before he slammed the opening shut, I said, "Hey, asshole, here's my membership card. Now open the goddamn door!" as I held up my badge right in front of his eyes.

"You got a warrant?" he shot back.

"Yeah, I got it right here under my jacket. Wanna see? Open up, asshole!" The peephole slid closed. After about 10 seconds of what sounded like deadbolts being unlocked, the door opened.

"We don't want any trouble, officer." A fairly large man with a fat belly, he didn't exactly look fit. I knew I could take him if I needed to.

"I'm a detective, not an officer," I shot back. The man nodded and cautiously took a few steps backward.

I observed a large room with numerous shelves and racks displaying everything from videos, magazines, posters, and various sex toys. Another man, who appeared to be middle-aged, sat in a booth fronted by steel bars. He overheard my conversation with the doorman, eyeballing me curiously. A big sign above the booth read: **Erotica Fliks Open 24/7**.

Four other people stood looking around in various parts of the store. They seemed to all be leering at me. I had caused a scene. This isn't my usual approach to things, but I didn't feel like dealing with any bullshit and I'd be damned if I'd let some oversized door monkey push my buttons like I was some punk. I had a job to do.

The man behind the booth stepped out.

"Is there a problem, Detective? We haven't done anything wrong," he said calmly.

"What's your name, sir?"

"Frank Simone. I'm the store owner." Frank was close to my height, with graying hair.

"Detective Sandes, Seattle PD." I flashed my badge again. "What kind of business are you running here, Frank?"

"This is a private store for people who want high-quality adult products. You have to be referred by a member to get in here. We do that to keep out the weirdos. We try to keep it private."

"Yeah, whatever, Frank." Two of the people in the store, apparently enjoying themselves when I entered, decided to leave. They walked out rather quickly and seemed worried by my presence.

"Hey Frank, do you know a fellow by the name of Leo Johnson?" I noticed his eye seemed to twitch when I said that. The remaining two customers glared at me again. It seemed I was disturbing their fun time.

"I couldn't possibly remember the name of everyone who comes in here."

"So, I guess that means the answer is 'no' then," I said, suddenly wheeling around at the other two fellows in the store.

"What about any of you?"
They both looked at me, startled, and shook their heads no.

"That's enough, Detective. Come into my office, and I'll talk to you," Frank finally said. The remaining two customers decided it was time to leave, bolting quickly. Frank led me to his office behind his booth, closed the door, and sat down. "Have a seat."

"Thank you, but I prefer to stand. What do you know about Leo Johnson?" I asked, impatient to find out what he knew and get out of there.

"He comes in here now and then. That's all," Frank replied.

"What kind of items does he buy?"

"Just the normal stuff. Magazines, videos." Frank kept his cool gaze steadily focused on me.

"Is that all, Frank? You never noticed anything odd about him? Did he seem like he was in any danger at all?"

"No, sir. Why, has something happened to him?"

"Why would you think that?"

"Well, you just implied he was in danger. Doesn't seem like a huge leap to guess he's in some trouble. He was a decent guy from what I gathered. Seemed like a normal man with an average porno fetish, I guess. He was probably just looking to get away from the wife and kids." Frank gave a small, mirthless laugh.

"Hmm. You know, that smells like bullshit to me, Frank. Whaddya say we close this joint down for the day and go have a talk at my place? The station."

Frank stood, put his hands in his pockets, and rocked back on his heels. "All right, Detective. Enough. I first noticed him in here about six months ago. Eventually, I started to see him here several times a week. He'd browse for a long time before he made a purchase. After his fifth or sixth visit, he came in one day when there were no other customers in the store. He approached me at the booth, and he seemed uneasy about something. I asked if there was anything I could help him with. He looked at me and asked if I had any kid stuff."

"Are you telling me he was looking to purchase child pornography, Frank?"

"Yes, Detective, that is what I'm telling you."

"And did he, Frank?" I asked harshly.

"Of course not. I told him this wasn't that kind of place and to get the hell out. He said he was sorry."

"That was the last time you saw him?"

"No, he told me he would buy a bunch of stuff if I didn't kick him out. I told him he could shop here as long as he never brought up that subject again. After that, he didn't come in quite as often, but he still showed up once a month or so."

"When was the last time you saw him?"

"About two weeks ago."

"Frank, what exactly is the process for getting a membership here?"

"You pay a fifty-dollars fee every six months to be a member, but you have to come in with a reference card that someone gives you to do so. As I said, this is a private club."

"Did Johnson have a reference card?"

"Yes, sir."

"Did you ask him who gave it to him?"

"He showed me his reference card, but I can't remember which customer referred him."

Frank was hiding something, but I wasn't sure what exactly. That was okay. I had a feeling that this wasn't going to be my last visit to this hell hole.

"Alright, Frank. See? That wasn't so hard, was it? Don't plan on going out of town anytime soon. I may have additional questions for you." I started to leave but suddenly remembered something.

"One more thing. Is the way I came in the only way into this place?"

"Yes, the rest of this building is part of an apartment house. You can see it from the front street, but there are no entryways to it from this side of the structure. You have to go back around to the front entrance to access it." Strange, I thought. I felt sorry for whoever rented that apartment. On the other hand, maybe they considered themselves lucky. I snickered to myself.

"Ok, you'll hear from me if I need any more information. Have fun doing whatever the hell it is you do here."

I left and headed back to my apartment.

Chapter 4

Once home, I called the Clearview Police Department and requested to speak to someone in Evidence Collection. A woman answered.

"Evidence Collection. This is Dora."

I explained who I was. I had found out earlier that the Clearview Police Department had gathered some of K.C.'s hairs from her bedroom as DNA evidence. I requested to pick up some of these samples the next morning.

"Sure thing, Detective. I just need your badge number so I can verify your credentials. If they check out, the samples will be here for you to pick up in the morning," she said. I gave her my information.

"Remember, you'll need your badge and a picture ID to pick up these items," she said.

"Yes, understood. Thank you." I hung up the phone.

***

I awoke several hours later and called to see if my request had been processed. I was told it was ready to pick up. After a speedy shower and a quick gulp of coffee, I arrived in Clearview shortly after 6:45 a.m. I approached the officer at the front desk and explained who I was and what I needed. He directed me to the Evidence Collection Department. When I got there, I saw a woman sitting at a desk with a large stack of papers behind her.

"I'm Detective Sandes with the Seattle PD. I'm here to pick up some evidence I requested."

"I just need to see your ID and badge," the secretary said. I handed them to her, and she examined them. She handed me a clipboard.

"Okay, just sign off on this sheet, and they're all yours." She pulled a small cardboard box out of a locked drawer and handed it to me.

"Thank you," I said. I opened the box to confirm its contents—small blond hairs inside a sealed plastic bag.

I headed back to the crime lab to deliver the hairs. By the time I got through all the rush hour traffic and arrived downtown, it was almost 8:30 a.m.

"I've got something new for you," I said, handing Parker the evidence. He looked at me with extreme curiosity.

"Blond hairs. Do you think these are from the same person whose hairs were found on Johnson's body?" Parker asked as he looked inside the box at the bag.

"Possibly. Can you check it out for me?"

"Sure thing."

I proceeded back to my office and sat down to check my email. I saw the usual crap that I received regularly. One email stated that an employee in one of the office buildings next door had burned some popcorn in the microwave, and this had caused the fire department to come and force an evacuation of the building. Now, none of the employees were allowed to microwave popcorn in any of the precinct buildings. Jesus! Don't most microwaves have a popcorn button these days? How do you screw that up? I hate looking through email. I swear—since email was invented, filtering junk mail has taken away so much productive time. I clicked on the third message. It stated:

As of July 22, 2005, Phillip Rodriguez no longer works for the Seattle Police Department Database Management team. Please refer all future calls or inquiries to Information at 555-786-6545.

Who the hell was Phillip Rodriguez? I scanned the rest of my mail. As usual, there was nothing important. I continued comparing my notes studiously for almost two hours, looking for any new leads. Just when I started to feel a little weary from staring at the computer screen for so long, my desk phone rang. I picked it up.

"Sandes speaking."

"It's Parker. Guess what? Those hairs you gave me are a match to the ones found on Johnson's body. Is there anything else I can help you with?"

"No, not now. I'll contact you if something else comes up. Thanks again." I hung up. Now I had some real work to do, eager to connect the dots between K.C. and Johnson. K.C. had been with Leo Johnson, but where and why? I did not believe K.C. had been inside the apartment; otherwise more of her hairs or DNA probably would have been found there. The only evidence found had been on Johnson's body. I was unsure where to go next.

I'm going north of the border, to Canada. I should go to Vancouver, British Columbia. I knew I had no jurisdiction there, but

I had to figure out why Johnson had been interested in Vancouver. All those books he had, and that receipt. What was the name again? Oh yes, U-Store-It Express.

I called Larry on his cell phone to tell him my plans to go to Vancouver.

"Canada? What the hell you wanna go up there for?" he said.

"I've found some evidence that could prove quite vital to this case, and I believe there could be some leads up there."

"Look, John, I know you've been working hard on this case, but I can't see why you need to go up there. I'm sure if this evidence does exist, there are people up there already that can check it out."

"That may be, sir, but I'd still like to go and see for myself. I may be able to find something up there. I only need a few days." I was willing to argue this one out with him if need be.

"All right. Meet me in my office today at three, and we'll discuss it. I want to hear your findings so far, and we'll figure out what to do. I've got a conference call in five minutes so I need to go. See you this afternoon." He hung up before I could get another word in.

He didn't sound too thrilled about me leaving the country, especially when there was plenty of criminal activity going on here. However, if I played my cards right, I believed I could convince him that it would prove useful in cracking the case.

This case meant a lot to me personally, especially since it involved a child. I hated seeing reports of missing or dead children. I hated the word "missing" because of the lack of closure. My daughter had left, living so far off the grid that she practically was missing. I know it was my fault. How could I have let my daughter get pushed out of my life by my very own wife? Why didn't I stand up for her when she was growing up?

 I had not been a good father. A real father would have said, "She's my daughter, and you'll just have to deal with it if you want to stay married to me." I remember one time when Mallory was nine or ten years old. I was upstairs looking outside the window. We had a playpen in the backyard that locked from the outside. When Mallory was much younger, we used to keep her in there so she could play outdoors without our worrying that she would crawl out into the street, in case Samantha or I needed to go inside for a minute or two. Well, this particular day, Samantha and I had agreed to watch the neighbor's two children for an afternoon while they went out to lunch. As was our habit, we left the children in the pen and I had been watching them from the second-floor window. From there I watched as Samantha went outside and unlocked the gate, and I heard Mallory downstairs in the kitchen washing the dishes. At first, I thought that Samantha was letting the kids out to bring them into the house, but I saw her let the two toddlers crawl out of the pen a short distance alone toward the driveway. What was she doing? I saw her walk around the side of the house and back toward the driveway to grab the kids. The next thing I knew, I heard the door slamming and Samantha yelling at Mallory. I rushed downstairs to see what the commotion was all about. I saw Samantha holding the two toddlers in her arms, arguing with my daughter.

"You left the gate unlocked, Mallory! How could you forget? After all, I've done for you, this is how you repay me? You are so damned selfish!" Samantha yelled at her.

"Honey, what are you talking about? I saw you—" I was quickly interrupted.

"Oh John, she's been pulling shit like this ever since we got together! Why do you let her get away with this? She needs discipline!" She continued shouting. Samantha raised her hand and was about to hit Mallory before I stopped her. I was dumbfounded. Did Samantha not realize that it was she who had opened the gate? She certainly had not done it on purpose. Had she?

"Dad, I didn't do it, I swear. Dad, pleease believe me," Mallory pleaded as she started to cry.

Samantha screamed, "You go to your room, young lady! There will be no supper for you tonight!" Mallory stared at me, clearly frightened.

There it was. That look. I will never forget that look. It was a look that said, "You know I didn't do this, Dad. Please don't let her punish me for it. She walks all over me just because she doesn't like me. She doesn't like me because she is jealous that you love me, Dad." I could read all that information in just one look from her. Instead of defending her like a good father would have done, I looked at Mallory and said very softly, "Please do what your mother says, Mallory."

"She's not my mother! No! Dad! Pleeease!" Mallory wailed. I had been weak, wanting to avoid any confrontation with my wife.

For some reason, I couldn't face Samantha and what she had done. I was never good with arguments in our marriage. Although I could have a mean temper from time to time, especially at my job if I felt things were not going right, I had always been a passive husband. I loved Samantha so much that I hated arguing with her. Thinking back now, I wish I had stood up more often for the way I felt about things. What Samantha had done that day worried me, but then I quickly forgot about it. I didn't stand up for Mallory when I should have. It's easy to get lost in thoughts about the past, but now I snapped back into reality. I wasn't going to let Larry talk me out of doing what needed to be done.

Chapter 5

July 22, 3:00 PM

"I don't see any reason why I need to send you up there, John. I mean, you can give the authorities the information by phone, right? What exactly have you found?" Larry sipped coffee from a mug.

"I believe the victim may have done some traveling to Vancouver. I have a hunch, and I feel it's worth looking into. I also believe the investigation would go more quickly and smoothly if I were physically there, rather than talking to someone on the phone. I think we'll save time and get to the bottom of this."

Larry raised his eyebrows at me as if to say, *you're nuts*. Instead, he remained silent for what seemed like a whole minute.

"Well, I guess investigating up there for a day probably wouldn't hurt if you want to go. Just make sure you work with the Canadian authorities. I know how you get, John. You don't need to do it all by yourself. You have resources, you know. Just remember to use them once in a while."

"Yes, of course. Anything it takes to get this resolved, sir," I said as he nodded.

"When are you going to head up there?"

"This evening. I'll probably stay all day tomorrow. I'll get back as soon as I can."

"Please do, John. We need you here. We're short enough on manpower as it is."

Funny, I didn't think we were struggling that much. I mean, times were busy, but criminal activity didn't seem to be higher than usual. I assumed that what Larry was referring to was the fact that the police department was short on staff that knew what they were doing.

"I'll be back ASAP. I promise."

"Well, go get 'em, ol' man," Larry laughed loudly. He swallowed the rest of his coffee in one gulp before slamming the mug back down on his desk. He had a big smirk on his face.

I exited expressing nothing but a slight nod, feeling slightly dumbfounded by Larry's quirky sense of humor. I swear, sometimes he acted like everything was a big joke. Larry was a good man, though. The jokes were just for show. Inside the guy was tough as a bull.

I got into my car and went home to quickly pack for my trip. I got a small suitcase, gathered some clothes and other personal hygiene items, and tossed them inside before I left. Half an hour later I was driving northeast, merging onto the highway. I surfed the radio stations. Nope, nothing good to listen to. I reached under the seat for my small CD holder and pulled out my favorite Neil Diamond album.

When I arrived in Vancouver, I checked into a Howard Johnson hotel. I connected my laptop to the internet and checked my email. After I finished, I headed over to the address of the U-Store-It Express.

The destination was about a twenty-minute drive from the hotel on the outskirts of the city. I noticed that the more I drove that the area was growing more remote and wooded, with trees on both sides of the road. Eventually, I saw a large open metal gate with a sign: **U-STORE-IT EXPRESS, OPEN 24/7**

A long dirt road went straight back for what seemed like miles, storage buildings lining both sides.

"Good God! There must be hundreds of units in this place," I said. The place was huge and no other cars or people were in sight. I drove through the maze for a few minutes, looking around before finally parking in front of one of the units. Where to start?

How the hell was I going to find Johnson's storage unit? Wait, I remembered that I had brought the ring of keys found on Johnson's night table. I took it out of the glove compartment and started flipping through them. There were nine keys on the ring. One was a Ford car key, and another looked like it might be his apartment key. The rest were inscribed with letters and numbers. I'd just have to try them all. I walked over to one of the storage units. It appeared to be about twelve feet tall by twenty feet wide. The door was designed to slide up and down like a garage. Looking at the padlock that secured the front of the door, I tried inserting the rest of Johnson's keys to see if any of them would even come close to fitting. One did fit into the padlock. I tried to turn the key and, of course, it did not turn because it was to a different storage unit. I had figured out what key to use, but which unit did it unlock? I looked at the key and read the number. 1067. I had to find Unit 1067. I looked closely at the unit I was standing in front of. The number above the door was 332. Since the numbers were in such small print and the day was getting darker, I couldn't drive and read the numbers from my car. I decided to just explore on foot.

After searching for about thirty minutes, I found 1067. I must have walked at least half a mile. I was surprised it didn't take me longer. I inserted the key into the lock and hoped luck was with me. Yes! It turned. Gripping the handle, I lifted the door. Holy shit! I was taken aback by what I saw. What a bunch of crap. There was stuff everywhere. Boxes, screwdrivers, hammers, saws, more work tools, benches, and furniture filled the unit. This could take forever.

"Jesus," I sighed, looking all around. I contemplated for a minute or two.

"Well, the hell with it," I finally said. I decided to start at the top and work my way down. I quickly put on my gloves in case I found something that needed to be analyzed for prints. I immediately started grabbing boxes, digging through everything that I could get my hands on, and not particularly caring whether I kept everything neat or not. Johnson wasn't coming back from the dead, so it didn't matter one way or another if I ransacked the place.

A couple of hours later, I'd gone through numerous boxes and other items and made absolutely no progress. I thought about ending my search and just cramming all the crap back in however I could. I had rummaged through a large portion of the unit. The objects in boxes up front were most likely to be the ones used recently, and I had already searched through most of those. My head started to throb. Goddamn headaches. They never cease. I pulled a packet of Tylenol out of my jacket pocket and swallowed two tablets. I stood still and took a couple of deep breaths. Despite feeling tired and having found no evidence, I pushed on. Another hour later, only a few rows of boxes in the back remained. The first box revealed some sort of large metal object behind it. Whatever it was, it was huge. I was curious as to what this object could be and focused my attention on it as I started to move the remainder of the boxes out of the way.

Once I cleared the rest of the boxes out, I got a better look at the object. It measured about eight by three feet. It looked like it was some sort of vault. Made of solid steel, it had two keypads with numbers spaced evenly apart along the front. Perhaps it had been purposely put toward the back to conceal it. It seemed odd to me to have something such as this here. What the hell was it for?

I pressed one of the number buttons and heard a beep. A red light blinked. I wonder what it could be. How the hell was I supposed to get inside this thing? It looked too secure to even shoot a hole through. My gun would only make a sizeable dent. I started punching in random numbers on one of the keypads. *Beep… Beep… Beep…* The red light blinked again. I could see a green light on each pad, as well. I did not know for sure how it worked, but it was similar to one I owned and I knew the light would turn green when the correct code was entered.

This was one hell of a safe. You didn't buy these at Wal-Mart. The safe that I owned required a four-digit code to be unlocked. What could the code to this safe possibly be? I figured I was going to have to get someone to cut through the damn thing with an acetylene torch. I was about to make some phone calls to the Vancouver PD to see if I could get some help busting this thing open. I hesitated. I should have called them before coming there, but I had chosen not to. I should have followed proper protocol, but I'd worry about the consequences later.

I looked at the vault again in wonder. All of a sudden, I remembered something I'd found in Johnson's apartment—something I happened to have brought with me. I raced back to my car, leaving the open storage unit unattended, sure there was no one else in the vicinity who could tamper with anything. Several minutes later, I opened the glove compartment and pulled out *Conceptual Physics*. It wasn't the book that interested me, but rather what was inside. There it was—the homemade bookmark with the Roman numerals on it.

XXX XX XVIII XV

It was a long shot but worth a try. I went quickly back to the vault. I looked at the bookmark again. 30, 20, 18, and 15. I punched a set of numbers on the left-front number lock: 3,0, 2,0…*beep…beep…beep…*. The red light blinked and beeped before I had a chance to enter in any more numbers. Well, this at least confirmed that the vault required a four-digit sequence. But what could the order be? Hmm. Think, John, think. I was going nuts. Calm down. I walked over to the keypad on the right and entered the same sequence: 3, 0, 2, 0. Ha! I heard the mechanism unlock, the green light on that side blinked once, and I pushed the handle down.

One side was now unlocked. I tried to see if I could pry it open just a little bit so I could take a peek. I lifted hard with no luck. I had to get the other side open. I went back to the other keypad and punched in 3, 0, 2, 0. No. Then I tried 1, 8, 1, 5. Nope. I tried 2, 0, 3, 0. Damn, that wasn't it either. Let's see, how about 3, 0, 1, 5? No. Okay, how about 1, 5, 1, 8? Yes! The green light came on, and I heard the unlocking sound. I pulled the handle down and lifted the lid, adjusting my grip to accommodate its weight. Inside lay a big black zippered bag. I felt something heavy wrapped within. Oh, no. I had gotten too wrapped up in my excitement in trying to open the vault. I paused a moment, preparing myself for what I knew I would find next. Unzipping the bag let out a stench that made me cover my nose and mouth so I wouldn't gag. I continued unzipping the bag with my free hand. Something large inside was wrapped in a blanket. I carefully removed the blanket, and… *Damn!*

Chapter 6

I slipped from the shock and bruised my leg when I saw the child-sized corpse in the blanket. I knew in my gut that this was K.C. Wingate. I closed the lid, grabbed my cell phone, called the Vancouver police, explained who I was and what I had found. The police arrived within minutes. I could tell that they suspected at first that I had something to do with the dead body. After I showed them my badge and answered all their questions, they knew what was going on. By the time I finished talking with them, it was nearly 11:00 p.m.

The Vancouver detective, Miller, grilled me about why I hadn't called them first, emphasizing that I was out of my jurisdiction and country. He said I should have called and told them my purpose for coming up before searching through the storage unit. I knew that this was exactly how they would react, but I was the one who had found the body, and that's all I cared about. I made sure to emphasize this to them. I probably would have wasted a lot more time if I had gone through all the bureaucratic red tape with the local police before going to the storage locker. After I pleaded my case to Miller, he seemed to dismiss my mistakes regarding protocol. They had a dead body to examine, and that was all that mattered. The police removed the corpse and taped off the area.

"We need to talk some more, Detective Sandes. Get some rest tonight and then meet me in my office tomorrow morning. I'll have my people deal with the rest of this here." He handed me his business card.

I didn't want to argue and decided to go back to my hotel and get some sleep. I had given Miller a sample of K.C.'s hair and was told the autopsy would be scheduled for tomorrow and that I'd get the details in the morning. I agreed and left, not feeling any better about the way things had turned out. I phoned Larry and briefed him on my discovery. He was flabbergasted that I had uncovered the body of the missing girl. He told me to get some rest, cooperate with the Vancouver Police, and do whatever I needed to do. After I hung up the phone, I tried to get some rest. I kept picturing the dead child in my mind. I tossed and turned in bed for a long time before finally drifting to sleep.

As usual, I woke up bright and early on Saturday. I looked over at the clock. It was 6:10 a.m. I was supposed to meet Miller in an hour at Vancouver Police Headquarters. I quickly got up and headed off. Once I got there, an officer at the main desk directed me down the hall to Miller's office.

Peering from behind his wide desk, Miller greeted me.

"Detective Sandes, I know I sounded gruff with you last night, but I want to let you know how grateful we are that you were able to find the body. We've confirmed the identity. She is K.C. Wingate. We got a positive match on her dental records, along with the information and DNA from the hairs you provided last night. We also found dried semen on the girl's body."

Oh, God. What had she gone through? Had she been raped by the killer? Was it Leo Johnson's?

"Is there any other information you could provide regarding this? What about this Leo Johnson fellow you told us about?" he asked.

"The news just gets worse, doesn't it? I'm not quite sure how he's involved, but that would be the place to start. Was the medical examiner able to determine how she died?" I asked.

"She was strangled. Even though the body had decomposed significantly, fractures were found on her thyroid cartilage."

"That's horrible. I'll call and have the investigation records from the Johnson case faxed here to you ASAP."

"Good, the sooner the better. Well, at least the girl's parents will know what happened. It's not good news, but there will be some sort of closure. Our forensics unit started the autopsy this morning. Once they're done and finish the report, we'll have the body transferred back to Seattle."

"Wait, shouldn't you have called the girl's parents before doing the autopsy?"

"Your boss already did. Larry left me a message on my voicemail this morning. From what he says, they were ready to drive up here immediately from Seattle. He persuaded them not to and assured them that the investigative process would be more effective if our team could analyze her body without interruption. We should have everything we need within forty-eight hours."

"How horrible for the parents," I said.

"Yes, it is. Unfortunately, the only thing we can do now is to find her killer."

"You're right. I'm gonna do everything in my power to make sure we find him. Thank you for your cooperation, Detective Miller. If you find anything else that you feel is pertinent to the case, please let me know."

"I will, Detective Sandes," he said.

I had talked with Miller for nearly two hours. As I drove back to Seattle, I thought about what to do next. I knew I needed to pay a visit to K.C.'s parents once I returned.

July 24

I was sitting in my office late in the afternoon thinking about the events that had occurred over the weekend. I'd visited K.C.'s parents the day before to tell them how sorry I was for their loss. The death of a loved one is always hard—particularly when it was a child. I could still picture the sad faces of K.C.'s parents when I had talked with them previously.

Later on that day I returned to my desk and continued to think while I sipped my coffee. I finally had shown the Wingates the picture of K.C. I'd found in Johnson's apartment. Mrs. Wingate immediately recognized the background in the picture. It had been taken in front of K.C.'s elementary school, but neither one of them had taken the picture. If that was true, could Johnson have taken the picture? And why? They were pretty upset enough the first time I visited, the week before, but that was nothing compared to what it was like on this last visit. My heart went out to them. Mrs. Wingate cried uncontrollably, while Mr. Wingate tried to comfort her as best as he could. They thanked me and told me how grateful they were.

Now at least they knew what had happened. I told them I would do everything in my power to get to the bottom of this and find out why. Driving home, I let the tears flow as I thought of my daughter.

Later on, back at the station, I was sitting at my desk thinking more about the previous day's events when my phone rang.

"Sandes."

"Detective Sandes, it's Parker."

"Hey, Parker. What ya got?"

"I just got off the phone with the Vancouver police. I sent them samples of Leo Johnson's DNA, and they matched those to the semen sample that was found on the little girl's body," Parker said rather sorrowfully.

I couldn't speak. What the hell was going on? Johnson had raped K.C. but had been killed himself. Who would have gone after him? I didn't think it could be one of K.C.'s parents. Neither one of them had reacted when I showed them the picture of Leo Johnson. No, a lot more pieces had just been added to this puzzle.

"Detective, are you still there?" Parker asked. I was getting lost in my thoughts again.

"Yeah. I know none of us wanted to hear any of that, but thanks for the information. I'll contact you if I need you." I instinctively slammed down the phone. Goddamn, bastard! How the hell could someone do this to a child? This makes my blood boil.

My desk phone rang again. By now I was even more frustrated. I let it ring a few times, trying to calm myself before I picked it up.

"Yeah," I said mechanically. It was Jimmy, a dispatcher from the front desk.

"Detective Sandes, I've got Officer Springer on the phone. He says it's urgent."

"Jimmy, can you have someone else take it? I'm busy right now."

"You're the only detective in the building right now, sir. There is no one else," Jimmy replied. Christ! Where the hell were people when you needed 'em?

"Ok, I'll take it. Thanks," I said reluctantly. I paused a moment while Jimmy patched him through. "What is it, Springer?"

"I'm at the Green Ridge Hotel. A man's body was found in one of the rooms. It was reported by Mrs. Dolores Glass, the hotel manager. One of the maids found the body. I just got here about ten minutes ago. I need somebody up here."

"I'll get right down there." After being briefed with the information, I told him to seal off the area and sit tight until I got there, hung up, and headed to the hotel. I wanted to work more on the Johnson case, but duty called.

***

Approaching the hotel's front desk, I asked to speak with Dolores Glass. A few minutes later a middle-aged, brown-haired woman emerged from the back and I introduced myself.

"Oh, thank goodness you're here, Detective! Bela Sanchez, one of our maids, found him this morning. Nobody remembers hearing or seeing anything unusual during his stay here. We have no idea when it may have happened," she explained.

"Where's the room?"

"Follow me. It's number 412."

I decided to contact Parker and his crew so they could meet me at the hotel. As Dolores led me to the crime scene, I called his cell phone. "Parker, I got a homicide at the Green Ridge Hotel and need you up here. Come to room 412 when you and your team get here."

Dolores stopped just outside the room. Crime scene tape had been strung across the entrance. Officer Springer, a short, burly man in his early forties, was standing next to it. Gesturing toward the door, Mrs. Glass said, "He's in there on the bed."

"Springer, just keep an eye out and don't let anyone in here who's not authorized," I said. He nodded.

I entered the room while Dolores waited outside. A man, whom I estimated to be in his late thirties to early forties, black hair with pale skin, was sprawled on the bed, a bullet hole centered in his forehead. I studied the body. Based on the look of his condition, he didn't appear to have been dead for long. I took a poke around the room. About fifteen minutes later Parker arrived with the forensics team. They photographed the body along with the rest of the apartment before we touched anything. The body was searched, and a wallet was found in his back pocket. His driver's license revealed him to be Randy Limehouse, thirty-nine years old, a resident of New York. He had checked himself into the hotel room approximately two days ago. The bullet hole reminded me of the one found in Leo

Johnson's forehead. Coincidence? Or could these two murders be connected? All of a sudden, my head began to pound.

"Does anyone have any aspirin or Tylenol?" I said aloud.

"Here you are, Detective." A young female technician handed me a small packet of tablets. I swallowed the pills and started to feel better within five minutes. The headaches seemed to just come and go without warning.

An hour later I was finished searching for prints and evidence. I asked Parker what he and his team had found.

"The bullet hole and location look almost identical to the one that was found in Leo Johnson. There were no signs of a struggle and no other marks on the body," he told me. I flipped through Limehouse's wallet and found a small wad of bills, debit and credit cards, and some business cards, all with Manhattan addresses. I left the room to find Ms. Glass at the front desk.

"Ms. Glass, did anyone hear gunshots during Mr. Limehouse's stay here?"

"No, none at all, Detective," she said.

I was once again puzzled. "What about the maid who found the body, Bela, is she here? I'd like to talk to her."

"Why, yes, Detective. She's been pretty shaken up all morning. I told her to take a break until you arrived." A tall, blond woman in a maid's outfit walked down the far side of the hallway. "Marcie, have you seen where Bela went to?" Ms. Glass said loudly.

"I just saw her a few minutes ago. She said she was heading out to the pool to sit and smoke," Marcie replied.

Ms. Glass nodded at Marcie before quickly leading me back downstairs to the main lobby. She directed me to the outdoor patio area where the pool was located. There I saw a short, thick Hispanic woman in her early thirties trying to light a cigarette. Her hands were trembling so badly that she kept missing the end with the flame. I approached her directly.

"Allow me, Miss Sanchez," I said as I took the lighter and ignited the butt for her. She took a long inhale for what seemed like an eternity before finally letting the smoke release out her mouth. This seemed to relax her, if only slightly.

"Miss Sanchez, my name is John Sandes. I'm a police detective. Did you see anyone leave Mr. Limehouse's room or anyone suspicious walking around during the time that he stayed here?"

"No. No. I knocked on the door and when he no answer, then I go in. I just found him in bed. Like that." She spoke with a thick accent. Though her English wasn't perfect, I could understand her fine. She mumbled some Spanish words, still shaking. I reached inside my coat pocket and handed her my business card.

"Here's my card. If there's anything you remember or think I should know, please call me." She nodded as I handed it to her. "I think maybe they should let you go home now."

I led her back to the front desk and talked with Ms. Glass again. I made sure that they let Bela leave, and I did another thorough search through Limehouse's room before heading downtown to Larry's office.

When I got there, he was sitting in his leather chair drinking a large cup of Starbucks coffee.

"John, glad you stopped by. Hey, don't you think Starbucks is the best damn thing in the world?" he said, pointing to the cup at the logo with the familiar goddess wearing the crown.

"Uh, yeah, it's good stuff, Larry. Look, I wanted to go to New York for a few days." I wasn't in the mood for any small talk, ready to get right to the point.

"Oh, yes, the Limehouse case. Don't worry, John. I already called the NYPD and filled them in on the details. They're pursuing every possible lead in this investigation. All you need to worry about is focusing your efforts here. Besides, you just got back from your road trip to Vancouver. You don't need to be traveling all over the place. That's what the feds are for. Don't worry. This time I'll make damn sure nobody misses anything."

"Well, Larry, I'd prefer to take a look for myself because—"

He quickly cut me off. "Yes, I know you feel like you have to run all over the place like Carmen Sandiego, but just have faith, ol' man. Other people do their job too, you know. Trust me, I'll keep you informed. I also gave the detective who's working the case in New York your phone number, in case he finds something. Just keep up the good work."

July 28

Parker had called me on Tuesday, informing me that the bullet that killed Limehouse was indeed from a .45 ACP handgun, the same weapon that had killed Leo Johnson. Since I'd spoken with him, I'd been working diligently on both investigations trying to piece the loose ends together, with absolutely no results. Dead end after dead end. No clues, nothing to go on. I called associates and friends of Randy Limehouse but came up with nothing. Nothing led to nowhere. Anything equals anywhere. Nothing equals nothing.

Damn it! Why couldn't I focus? I was going crazy over this case. To make matters worse, Samantha had been leaving nasty voicemails on my cell phone lately. She had just broken up with the guy she was seeing, and this led to her increasing her meds. Lucky for me, I thought. She had more medication than she knew what to do with. Most of it she didn't even need. She took it because she liked to feel drugged, pure and simple. She had so many damn painkillers—Vicodin, Percocet—you name it, she had it.

At that instant, my cell phone rang. I looked at the caller ID. Samantha again. I decided not to answer. After a moment my phone beeped, alerting me that I had a voice message. What the hell does she want now? I decided I would just ignore it. A minute later I was unable to resist the urge. Christ! I picked my phone up and dialed into my voicemail to listen to the message:

"John, I hope you're having fun up there dilly-dallying, playing policeman or whatever it is that you do. Oh, John Sandes, to serve and protect. What makes you think you can protect anyone when you didn't even know how to take care of me? Oh, John, really I do wish you would do something more constructive with your life. Besides, don't you think you're a little old for this? You have to realize your limitations. Anyway, the reason I'm calling is that I'm a little short on money for the bills this month. I've been having this abdominal pain lately. My doctor told me that he couldn't find anything wrong, but after I persisted, he told me I should try this new medicine. Look, I know that you just sent a check two weeks ago, but they also raised the prices of prescriptions and—"

I'd had it with her. I wasn't listening to any more of her bullshit. I got so worked up that before I realized it, I had launched my phone full speed at the door. I bent over to pick it back up, luckily it didn't have any damage. As soon as I stood back up I suddenly felt queasy. Samantha's voice echoed in my skull: *"You didn't even know how to take care of me! That's right! Run away from all your problems!"* Then came Mallory's voice. *"No! Dad, I didn't do anything wrong! Please! Samantha hates me, Dad. You know I'd never do the things she says I do."* Everything went black….

Chapter 7

I awoke in a hospital bed. My head was sore, and I felt groggy.

"John, buddy, are you okay?"

I could see Larry looking over me. "What happened?" Confused, I looked around. Where was I?

"You took a pretty hard fall there this morning. Everyone outside your office heard you. Penny said she was walking by and saw you throw your phone against the door. When you passed out, you somehow managed to knock over your computer monitor, and it shattered into a zillion pieces."

"Damn. My ex got me riled up." I sat up, eager to get out of the bed.

"Whoa, there, fella. Take it easy. Just stay put for right now." Larry placed his hand on my shoulder. "Listen, John, the doctor thinks you're going to be fine, and she said she'd let you go later today if you felt okay. She said your blood pressure was very high. I know you've been under a lot of stress lately. Have you been eating right and drinking enough water?"

"I've skipped some meals during the last few weeks, but I'm fine."

"Ok, that's it. I'm officially giving you a two-week leave of absence. No arguments, pal. You need to rest."

I finally got out of bed and sat in a nearby chair facing the TV. We watched the news while I ate some food from the small meal tray a nurse had left earlier. On the screen, a familiar anchorman spoke:

"You're watching King Five News. Earlier this week, a thirty-nine-year-old male was found dead at the Green Ridge Hotel. So far authorities have no information as to who—"

Larry reached up and turned off the television. "Okay, that's enough. You don't need to deal with any of that shit right now," he said gruffly.

Two hours later, after eating tasteless food and lying around like a damn vegetable, I was released from the hospital. When I spoke to the doctor, she said my stress level was high, and skipping meals only made it worse for a man my age. Before he left, Larry told me that perhaps I should just retire now rather than waiting till the end of the year.

He'd mentioned retirement to me several times over the past few years, but I felt that I had done my job well enough during that time to continue till the very end. I think Larry may have sensed that I had started to slip recently. As much as I tried to hide it, he knew about my frequent headaches and aching knees. Nevertheless, I refused to listen to any of this nonsense about retiring until my mandatory date. I kept telling Larry and myself that I felt fine most of the time even if I didn't.

When I arrived back at my apartment, I watched the news for a couple more hours, then fixed myself a sandwich. Shortly after that, I got into my bed, listening to some music before finally drifting into a deep sleep.

***

I'm standing in the backyard at my Long Island home in East Quogue. It's a cool Saturday afternoon in the spring of 1981. The neighborhood is quiet, birds are chirping in the background, and the trees are moving with the wind. I take a long deep breath, enjoying the fresh air. I look out at our swimming pool; it still has its cover on. With summer approaching, I know that it'll need some maintenance. I glance up at the bright blue sky, looking intently at the clouds and getting lost in my thoughts. I suddenly hear a loud bark. No one else is home except for me and Dennis, our black Labrador retriever. Dennis, a female dog with a male name, is standing next to me. She is gazing at the tennis ball I have in my hand, trying to determine when and where I will throw it. I heave it across the backyard, and she sprints after it. She fetches the ball and races back to me. When I try to take it from her mouth, she won't let go.

"How do you expect to play fetch if you won't give it back, dummy?" I laugh at her. She lets out a low, playful growl. She hesitates before finally letting me pull it out from between her teeth, although not without a fight.

"Hi, John. How you doin'?" a voice calls. It's our neighbor Al sitting on his back porch, smoking his pipe.

"Hi, Al. Enjoying the day?"

"Oh, yeah. This is the best type of weather."

Al's wife died several years ago and he lives alone, with no pets. All his attention and care are devoted to his extensive medieval armor collection. His house is like a museum with walls displaying his range of swords and shields, each polished to a meticulous shine. Life-sized suits of armor appear to guard the treasures. I don't understand how he can live by himself with all that spooky stuff around. He has to be lonely, and I feel sorry for him. I'm so thankful that I have a family. Dennis barks again, eager for me to throw the ball.

"I'll talk to you later, Al. Why don't you come over for dinner tonight?"

"I may take you up on that." He smiles and waves, continuing to smoke his pipe.

I throw the ball again and this time chase after it as well. Dennis quickly beats me to it. I continue to chase her. I managed to grab hold of her. I slip and fall on the dirt. She jumps on top of me, licking my face. "Stop it, you silly dog," I say, laughing. She pounces on my stomach. I keep laughing. I am so happy.

Chapter 8

July 29

I slept until almost 10 a.m., which was rare; I must have needed the rest after all the excitement of yesterday. Larry had given me two weeks' leave, and I was officially off any cases I'd been working on. I complained, stating that I would be back to full strength after a couple of days' rest, but he wouldn't bend. I also knew that I would not be able to win the argument about going to New York. I could tell Larry was serious about what he said yesterday at the hospital. Damn. *What the hell am I gonna do for two weeks, when there's still work to be done?* This case had reenergized me and I felt more alive than I had in months.

Wait a second. Suddenly a thought occurred to me. Larry suggested I go somewhere and take a vacation. Who the hell was gonna know whether or not I went to New York? Of course, Larry would probably find out eventually, but, if I was careful, I might be able to get a look at Randy Limehouse's residence. Hell, it sure beats sitting on my ass for two weeks. I hurried and packed enough clothes to last me for a few days, then I called the airlines to book the next available flight to New York.

I exited the gate at LaGuardia at 10:45 p.m. I had booked a flight with Delta Airlines at 2 p.m. Pacific time and arrived at Denver at approximately 5 p.m. Mountain Time, with an hour layover in the airport, finally arriving in LaGuardia National Airport in New York a few hours later. I was exhausted. I had not bothered to book a return flight because I had no idea how long it would take me to get my work done. I would have been lying to myself if I'd said I wasn't a little bit worried. Regardless, I was going with my gut feeling on this. If I got punished, then the hell with it. They could fire my ass. If that happened, I would be content—at least I'd done everything I could. I'm practically done with my career anyway. What the hell did I have to lose this late in my life? I booked a room at a Holiday Inn in Manhattan.

Chapter 9

July 30, 7:00 a.m.

Limehouse had lived in a condominium complex. This was good because I could just go to the main office building and request entry, bypassing the NYPD altogether. Anything that would keep Larry from knowing that I was in New York was good. Hopefully, the condo office was open on Sundays. I took the subway and got off approximately three blocks from his condo building. As the subway doors closed behind me, a young attractive woman I could tell was a hooker stared as I turned a street corner.

"Hey Mista, you want some company?" After so many years in this field, I could spot them a mile away. I waved her off without so much as a glance. A few minutes later I was facing Laketon Condominiums, gazing through the front entrance gate. Not a luxurious structure, but nice. The building was about twenty stories tall and I could see that each of the units had a screened-in balcony.

I made my way to the office. I was in luck—it was open. I approached a young woman who appeared to be in her early twenties.

"Hello miss, I'm Detective Sandes. I'm investigating the death of Randy Limehouse. I'd like to see the inside of his residence."

She stared at me with a puzzled look. "No one informed me about anyone coming today. Can I see some identification, please?"

I held out my badge and ID.

"Sorry, Detective. I just had to make sure. They told us they were done investigating the place, and that a relative would come tomorrow morning to collect the rest of his stuff." She hadn't bothered to check my ID too closely, since it showed that I was from out of state.

"I'm sorry for the trouble. We just have to look over a few more things. Sorry again for the short notice."

"That's okay. It's not like I have anything exciting to do around here anyway. It's 622 B. Follow me." She got up and walked past me.

"Thank you, ma'am."

She led me onto the elevator and up to the sixth floor. She proceeded down the hallway, stopped in front of Limehouse's door, and unlocked it. "If there's anything else you need just let me know, okay?" She walked away, back toward the elevator.

"Thank you, again."

The place was full of packed boxes, but most were not taped shut. I closed the door and started searching through them as quickly as possible. I didn't want to be there too long in case the NYPD did show up. I could suffer severe consequences for conducting an unauthorized investigation yet again. If I was going to play the rogue, I had to be cautious.

I found many books, business weekly journals, car repair guides, novels by an assortment of authors. I sifted through a box filled with manila folders, each labeled according to the subject, and found several containing past tax forms as well as one with warranties for purchases of electronics and appliances.

Even working as fast as I could, I had already spent two hours there. It could take days if I checked every scrap of paper.

Another folder held Limehouse's bank statements. As I reached up to place it on the stack of folders I had already examined, the folder slipped out of my hand and fell to the floor, scattering about a hundred sheets. As I picked them up, I found a photo that must have been buried among the rest of the contents of the stack. A Post-it note attached to the photo was scrawled with letters in red ink that read, "Phillip Rodriguez." It was a picture of a man who looked to be of Latino origin, late-twenties to early-thirties. There was also an address scribbled on it:

123 Foren Lane

Seattle, WA 18765

Phillip Rodriguez. Where had I heard that name before? I couldn't remember. I took a photo of the image and address with my phone.

I gave it another hour and finding nothing else of significance, concluded my search. I made sure to leave everything else that I had searched exactly the way I'd found it. I came back down the elevator into the office building. The young woman was organizing a large stack of papers at her desk

I returned to the office and thanked the young woman for her cooperation and then called a taxi.

Later I sat down with my computer to check my emails. I messaged Larry to let him know that I had gone out of town. He may have been trying to reach me at home to see if I was feeling better. Too much had been going on. I typed a short memo:

Larry,

I decided to leave the city for a few days. I need to clear my head. I guess it's a good thing you gave me the time off. When I get back to work, I should be at full strength.

John

I scrolled through the rest of my mail, both new and old. Suddenly I saw the email that triggered my memory when searching Limehouse's apartment:

As of 21 July 2005, Phillip Rodriguez no longer works for the Seattle Police Department Database Management team. Please refer all future calls or inquiries to Information at 555-786-6545.

I pulled out my phone to look at the photo I had taken of the image and address that I had found at the Laketon condo complex. It was the same name. It also happened to be a Seattle address. This didn't necessarily mean anything. Hell, there are probably hundreds of Phillip Rodriguez's. It's a fairly common name, I suppose. I figured I would check just to be sure. I could get his phone number from the employee directory in the internal system if it hadn't been deleted yet. I logged into the directory. Yes, there it was.

Name: *Phillip Rodriguez*
Address: *123 Foren Lane*

Seattle, WA 18765

Telephone: 555-786-8765

Holy shit. It was the same guy. I decided I would call this guy to inquire about his relationship with Randy Limehouse. I called Rodriguez's number. A woman answered the phone.

"Hello?"

"Hello. May I speak with Phillip Rodriguez please?"

"Uh, with whom am I speaking?"

"I'm Detective Sandes with the Seattle Police Department. I understand he worked in our organization until recently. I have a few questions I'd like to ask him."

"What are you talking about? Don't you know he's been missing for over a week?"

This case just got stranger by the minute.

"I...I... No. I'm so sorry. I had no idea. I didn't know him personally. I received an email stating that he no longer worked for our organization, but that's all I knew. Are you a family member?"

"I'm Lauren, his girlfriend."

"When was the last time you saw him?"

"Look, if you're a detective then you should already know this information." She didn't buy my story. By now I was even more perturbed and confused.

"Look, Lauren. I've been out of town. I'm working on another case out of state right now which may involve your boyfriend. I'm sorry about what happened, but please trust me. If you can give me any more information, I promise you that I will do whatever I can to help you. If you'd like, go ahead and call the police station and verify who I am."

There was a short pause.

"I'm sorry, Detective. I didn't mean to be rude. I guess I have nothing more to lose by talking with you. It's just that I've been so upset lately. Something awful must have happened to him."

"It's okay, Lauren. Just take a deep breath and tell me what exactly happened when he disappeared."

"He came home that day very upset. He told me that he had just been fired. I asked him what happened, and he said he was too upset to talk about it. He said he wanted to go visit his parents in Oregon. He left to see them the day after he was fired." She had changed her tone. I sensed that I had instilled some hope in her.

"What time did he leave?"

"He left in the morning sometime. Around eight, I think. I...I..." She started crying.

"Look, Lauren. I apologize. I know you must be very worried. I did not know about Phillip's disappearance until I called you just now. I had no idea about this case until just now. His disappearance will now be a part of my investigation, too. Do you remember who you spoke to about his disappearance?"

"Oh. There were two men. One of them was Detective Locke. The other's name I can't recall."

I couldn't recall anyone by the name of Locke at the Department. "Listen, Lauren. I know you've already been questioned about all of this, but would you mind talking with me sometime this week? I may be of some help to you. I'll be back soon, hopefully sometime within the next couple of days."

"Sure, when?"

"Would Tuesday work for you?"

"Yes. Tuesday would be fine, Detective."

***

It was 8:00 p.m. and all I could think about is that more and more of these cases were starting to resemble a jigsaw puzzle. What could Phillip Rodriguez and Randy Limehouse possibly have in common? I pondered the connection as I ate my dinner at a noodle shop. Examining the photocopy of the paper with Rodriguez's address, I noticed a small line of text at the bottom of the page that read:

Sent by 555-786-0098   9:11:49

It was a fax!

There was the number and the time it had been sent. Now I just needed to get back to my office and use the reverse directory to find out who's number it was. It didn't have a date specification; nevertheless, it might still be useful. I jammed the paper back into my coat pocket and finished my meal.

Chapter 10

Later that evening I took a stroll along Times Square looking in the windows of the closed shops. I saw a model train store. Oh, how I love trains. Ever since I was a little kid, trains have always fascinated me. I used to own hundreds of different model trains ranging anywhere from the 1950s to the early 1990s. It had always been fun to set up the train tracks all around the living room and have them go around the Christmas tree during the holidays.

Further down the block, there was a motorcycle shop. I used to own a bike. An '88 Honda Shadow. I had gotten rid of it ages ago. Those were happier times, before the darkness that had surrounded me. Those days were long gone.

Now all I had to concentrate on were murders, rapes, and violence. So many crimes were committed against innocent people. I had no real friends anymore and certainly no female companion. I hadn't had a relationship in several years. I did meet a woman once during my first year in Seattle. I met her through one of the investigations I'd been working on. Like most women I've been attracted to during my lifetime, she was a serious mistake. I had trusted her deeply, and she had deceived me. I eventually found out that she was not exactly who she appeared to be.

I've steered clear of any other romantic encounters while burying myself in my work. At times, I miss the married life that I once had. I miss watching M*A*S*H episodes on television with my family in the old house. I miss talking with my daughter.

A bookstore across the street caught my eye. It was still open, and I went inside to look around. Browsing through the bargain books, I picked up a large coffee table book about horses. Mallory used to love horses when she was a kid. She always had horse posters tacked up all over her bedroom walls and figurines of them on her shelves. I replaced the book on the shelf and left the store, continuing to stroll through the streets, haunted by a life I'd never have again.

I must have walked several blocks and lost track of the time. It had started raining heavily, and as I looked around, I realized I had no idea where I was. I had become completely lost in my thoughts. My watch said it was 11:30 p.m. As I turned a street corner trying to get my sense of direction, I saw three men appear from the alleyway.

"Hey, old man, have you got a dollar?" one of them asked me. I ignored him and kept walking, but one of the other men stepped in front of me.

"I don't think you heard my friend over there, Pops. He asked you a question," he said with a mean look in his eye.

"I don't have any. Now get out of my face." I wasn't in the mood for this bullshit. As I tried to step around the man, I was kicked in the back from behind and fell to the ground. I looked up and saw one of them staring down at me, a knife in his hand.

"Give us your fuckin' money now!" he yelled. The look in his eyes told me he was ready to do anything. I just stared at him. As he tried to lunge on top of me, I kicked him in the groin and his legs collapsed beneath him. As soon as I got to my feet, the third man punched me in the face, drawing blood. One man ran at me. I grabbed his wrists and was able to shove him into one of the others, knocking them both off-balance. The guy with the knife charged me, slashing wildly. I grabbed his hand and slammed it hard against the side of a building wall, breaking his wrist. He yelled out in agony and dropped the knife. I quickly pulled my .38 from its holster and pointed it at them.

"You wanna fight? Let's go, cause I'm gonna come out swingin', and I'm gonna swing hard, you bastards!" I yelled back.

"Shit! I never woulda guessed Pops had a piece. Let's get the fuck out of here!" one said as they all ran down the street. Jesus Christ! Another reason I don't miss New York. I went into the alley and sat down with my back against the wall. I felt the blood trickle down my face. It was still pouring down rain, and I was drenched, but I needed to sit for a moment. I seated myself on the ground. A minute later, I heard a yippy bark further down the alley and saw a small Jack Russell Terrier run toward me. It looked slightly timid, but it approached me anyway. I stared at it and held out my hand as it licked my fingers. It looked at me, whimpering with concern. It licked the blood on my face. I rubbed its head.

"Where'd you come from, little fella?" I looked at the dog's collar, which read:

Grace

a.k.a.

"SaberGrace"

555-987-8987

"Gracie, where are you? How'd you get out? Come here, girl!" I heard a woman yell from a doorway in one of the alley buildings. At that instant, the dog took off, presumably to its home.

It'd been so long since I'd had a dog. I love dogs. I don't have one now because I'm never at home. It's not right to have an animal if you can't spend time with it. I don't agree with those people who leave their dogs and cats outside all the time. Once I had some neighbors who always kept their dog chained in the backyard and ignored it. Sure, they left food out for it, but they never petted or played with the animal. Whenever I was mowing the backyard, I had to watch it staring back at me with this pitiful look that said, *please come see me.*

I sat there for a few moments longer. Eventually, I got up, and as I walked back, I felt my knees starting to ache. They'd been bothering me a lot. I kept meaning to see a doctor, but always put it off. I left the alley. I walked a couple more blocks and was able to hail a cab back to my hotel. I needed to save my energy and get some rest. Whatever was coming in this crazy case, it was going to take all my strength to get to the bottom of it.

Chapter 11

August 1, 7:30 a.m.

Ah, back—in my bed. Yesterday felt like a long day in hell. The flight back from New York to Seattle was long and exhausting. Before I left, I decided to contact the NYPD regarding Limehouse's murder. The odd thing was what had happened after I tracked him down and told him who I was. His name was Richard Greene, and although he had spoken with Larry, he had not been informed about me. When I arrived at the station, he asked for my identification. He explained to me that since I hadn't been authorized to investigate out there that I was out of my jurisdiction. I didn't tell him that I had already searched Randy Limehouse's condo or to mention the information I found regarding Rodriguez. Greene said that he would call Larry. I told him not to worry about it and that I would call him myself and headed outside. Instead, I took the nearest cab back to my hotel and packed my stuff, went to the airport, and took the earliest possible flight home.

    I didn't feel like answering the NYPD's questions. I was sure Greene called Larry when I failed to return. During the flight back, I checked my messages. I had two messages from Larry asking me to call him. His tone was rather rough. I knew then that I was in deep shit. My cover had been blown. What the hell was I supposed to tell him? I felt that I had to get to the bottom of this case no matter the consequences. I knew this was my last case. Mentally I felt as if I could go on forever, but physically, with all the headaches and knee problems, my body was wearing down. I got out of bed and brewed myself a pot of coffee. I'm not ready to talk to Larry yet, I thought. But I knew I couldn't put him off any longer. I finally picked up the phone and made the call, preparing myself for whatever came next.

"John, what the hell have you been doing? NYPD called me yesterday and told me you were up there inquiring about the Limehouse case. What in Christ's name is going on in your damn head?" He sounded pissed.

"I know, Larry. I'm sorry. I just couldn't get my mind off it. I know it was wrong. Look, I—"

"Goddammit, John!" There was a pause. Then he spoke again, more calmly. "Well, what did you find?"

"Nothing, sir. Nothing. I didn't get a chance to do anything except walk around the city for a little while before I talked to NYPD. It was a total waste of my time." I decided not to tell him about Limehouse's condo because if Larry knew, then he would have to tell the NYPD. I didn't feel like going through any more lectures on protocol. Besides, I didn't have any leads yet. When I found something relevant, I would tell him. I just hoped the lovely young woman at the Laketon Condominium complex hadn't decided to tell anyone that I had been there.

"Look, John. The reason I'm so upset is that I know you're sick. I can see it in you. Your eyes and even your body movements say it all. You need to take it easy. I don't want to be responsible for another seizure or whatever it was that you had. I know you, you're too damn stubborn to retire yet. I should probably order you to desk duty. That way you would still be contributing. What do you say to that?"

"Oh, Larry, I'm fine," I said.

"John, I'm serious. You either step down right now completely or we move you to paperwork."

I couldn't believe what I was hearing. This was it. What I had been dreading for a long time. What could I do?

"Uh, Larry. Look, I... Okay. Okay." I decided to agree so he would at least get off my back. I didn't want to continue arguing about it on the phone. But how could I do anything from a damn desk? Well, I had no other choice, did I? I was upset with myself. I had failed.

"John, look. I'm sorry I yelled. What do you say we meet for lunch? It's on me. I'd like to sit down and talk this over with you and discuss the details."

"Okay, Larry. Where should I meet you?" I wasn't particularly eager to go to lunch, but I felt it was best to smooth things over with him.

"How about the Library Bistro and Bookstore Bar? It's on the corner of Madison and Spring. They've got a nice outdoor courtyard. On a beautiful sunny day like this, it's perfect."

"What time?"

"One o'clock sound good?"

"See you then," I said and placed the phone back on its base.

***

It was 1:00 p.m. and I had just parked my car on my way to meet Larry. I inserted some quarters into the parking meter and walked toward Madison and Spring. As I approached the restaurant, I easily spotted him in his dark brown suit waiting for me at a table on the patio near the sidewalk. He looked relaxed, smoking a cigarette. I was relieved that by the time I got to the table he had finished. I can't stand the smell of smoke. I smoked for almost ten years. I started in my early twenties because it was considered hip back then, but after learning the pains of nicotine addiction, I quit.

"Hi, Larry," I said, seating myself.

"John. Good to see you." He sounded much calmer than when we spoke on the phone earlier.

"What can I get for you two gentlemen to drink?" the waiter said as he stopped at our table.

"Iced tea, please," I said.

"Diet Coke for me, thanks," Larry replied. The waiter nodded and walked off.

There was a moment of silence when I could feel him studying my face.

"Well John, have you thought about my offer?"

"Yes, I have, Larry."

Another pause. We stared at each other intently. I had thought about this question long and hard since this morning. I finally responded.

"Larry, I agree with you. I think it is time for me to step down into a supportive role with the police department. I'm too old to be chasing down thugs. As long as I can contribute in some way, even if it means sitting at a desk all day, I think I'd be satisfied. At least until my mandatory retirement date at the end of the year."

For a second, I made myself believe what I was saying. I had rehearsed that little speech several times after our chat this morning. I decided that although I would officially step down from the case, I had enough information to continue my investigation without Larry's knowledge. I had not been cautious enough when I had been in New York, but this time would be different. I didn't know what else to do. My heart was too deep inside this case. If I played my cards right, it would keep Larry from pressuring me all the time. Maybe if I found something relevant to the case, he would change his mind.

"John, I'm glad you've taken the time to think things through logically. You've done a great job over the last several years. You've had your share of cases, that's for sure. Do you remember the cat murders several years ago?"

"Yeah, I remember them. That was around my second year in the department." Larry had reminded me of the first truly bizarre case that I encountered. There had been a string of serial murders where each victim was found with a dead cat. The strangest thing about those murders was that none of the cats belonged to any of the victims. The killer was eventually revealed to be some wacko animal control employee who had picked up stray cats in the city and, for whatever reason, enjoyed killing the victims and the cats together. The killer had believed that by murdering the cat with the person his kill count increased since cats are supposed to have nine lives. He said doing this made him feel as if he had killed more people and that his victims' souls entered into his own body, providing him with more vitality. What a freak.

Larry and I ate and talked for the better part of the afternoon, reminiscing about all the good times as well as the bad over many years. Just as I took a big mouthful of spaghetti, I heard a woman's voice call my name from the street behind me.

"Detective Sandes, is that you?"

I wheeled my head around. It was Bela, the maid from the Green Ridge Hotel, accompanied by another Hispanic woman about the same age.

"Miss Sanchez. How are you?"

"Is good to see you, Detective. I been doing better. Sorry about the last time you come. I just scared, that's all." I couldn't help notice that her friend was staring at Larry.

"Pardon me for being so rude. This is Larry Wegmueller. Larry, this is Ms. Bela Sanchez. I don't believe I know your friend's name."

Bela continued with her slightly broken English, "This is Rosie. She work at the hotel also. We good friends." Rosie just looked at Larry and me, smiling. Her smile looked forced like she was nervous about something.

"Please forgive her. She no speak English much."

I nodded toward Rosie and gave her a warm smile. "Look, I'm no longer investigating the case. I'm not sure which detective is going to take my place. For the time being, I still want you to give me a call, and then, if need be, I will relay any information you have to whoever picks up this case." I glanced over at Larry to make sure that was okay. He nodded his head at me slightly.

"*Gracias,* Detective Sandes. I appreciate all you done. Is nice to meet you, Señor Larry." She and Rosie waved goodbye, and Rosie seemed to almost hide behind Bela as they walked away. Rosie gave us one last glance as they walked farther down the street.

Chapter 12

August 2, 4:15 p.m.

I parked my car in the driveway at 123 Foren Lane. I had meant to come sooner, but lunch with Larry lasted longer than expected. I thought about telling Lauren over the phone that I was no longer on the case, but I didn't want her to feel more discouraged than she already was. I'm sure my last phone call about Mr. Rodriguez had raised her hopes of finding him. I felt the least I could do was show up and talk with her in person. Rodriguez's home was a fairly large house in a nice, upper-middle-class neighborhood. I rang the doorbell. A young, slender blond woman answered the door. She looked very worried but was trying her best to act calm.

"Are you Detective Sandes?" she asked.

"Yes, ma'am. May I come in and talk with you?" I asked, showing her my badge.

"Please, come in."

"This is a nice house. How long have you been living with Phillip?" I asked.

"I moved in with him about three months ago. We had planned to get married sometime within the next year."

"Lauren, I found out recently that they're taking me off this case, but I promise you that I am still going to do as much as I can to assist you in getting Phillip back. The first thing I'd like to do is take a quick search around the house. Do you mind if I do that?"

"Sure, help yourself. Would you like something to drink?" she said as she started to rearrange items in the kitchen.

"No, thank you." I glanced around the house. "How long have you known Phillip?" I said as I walked up the stairs, speaking loud enough so that she could hear.

"We've been dating for almost three years." She hurried up the stairs to follow me. "What exactly are you looking for?"

"Oh, nothing in particular." Rodriguez had Microsoft certifications hanging up in his bedroom and a few computers on a small desk against a wall. I opened his walk-in closet and found a large collection of polo shirts and khakis on hangers, pressed perfectly. A huge stack of computer magazines sat on the floor—*PC World, Computer Shopper,* and *Hacker Quarterly* among others.

I looked around the inside of the closet some more and saw an unlabeled manila envelope propped against the wall behind some shoes. I opened it and saw that it was a porno magazine titled *Fantasy Xposure,* but it wasn't the title that grabbed my attention. When I flipped through the magazine a little white piece of paper fell out. It was a receipt. A receipt from Erotica Fliks, documenting a $14.95 purchase dated July 17. As I studied it, Lauren came up behind me.

"Oh, God, I can't believe he bought that stupid thing. I kept trying to get him to throw it out. I just don't understand men sometimes. I mean, why would he need this when he had me?"

"Do you mind if I take it?"

"Yeah. Whatever, take it. I don't want to look at that disgusting piece of trash. What you do with it is your business, Detective," she said with a slightly sarcastic tone. Great, now she thought I was some old perv.

"Oh, uh…no. Possible evidence."

I should probably go back to Erotica Fliks again and check things out just in case. Maybe Frank might know something about Phillip Rodriguez. Maybe Rodriguez and Johnson were somehow connected. I didn't see anything else in the bedroom that caught my eye. I took a quick look in the bathroom; everything looked in order. I went back downstairs.

"Lauren, was Phillip acting strangely or hanging out with anyone suspicious before he disappeared?"

"He did seem to be acting a little stressed out a few days before he was fired. Other than that, there was nothing that stood out."

"Did Phillip have any friends he liked to get together with?"

"Not too many, he was pretty much a loner. If he wasn't spending time with me then he was tinkering around with his computer upstairs. He was always upgrading or whatever they call it. Occasionally he hung out with a couple of his co-workers from the IT department, but not too often."

After I was done searching through the house, I told Lauren that I would call her if I found any information regarding the whereabouts of her boyfriend. I just hoped I sounded believable to Larry when I told him earlier that I would step down. He didn't specify what my exact role would be when I came back from leave.

The way I saw it, I wasn't doing anything wrong by just talking with Lauren. Nothing to worry about.

When I left Rodriguez's, it was almost 5:45 p.m. I headed back toward Magnolia to find the strange store I had visited only a week earlier. Damn. There was too much traffic. It was rush hour, and it could take a while. I decided to stop by the nearest Starbucks. It's not like I had to hurry. Erotica Fliks was supposedly open twenty-four hours. I walked into the shop and approached the counter.

"What can I get for you, sir?" a boy who looked to be about sixteen asked me.

"I'll take a small house coffee, please."

"Oh, you mean a tall?"

"Uh, yeah, tall. That's fine." Why couldn't they just say small, medium, and large and use proper English, for God's sake? By the time I sat down with my coffee, the sunny day had been replaced by sheets of rain. I looked out the window, sipping the coffee and reflecting on my past.

I remembered working in construction in my late twenties in New York. I spent a lot of time on scaffolding. While at first, the job seemed very intimidating due to the extreme heights, it paid well, and I decided that the risk was worth it. Samantha and I had been married for only about a year at that time, living in an apartment. Joan still had custody of Mallory, but I was hoping to finally become her legal guardian. It was evident that Joan was getting emotionally unstable. She had been diagnosed with a serious case of depression and wasn't paying much attention to Mallory. With me making more money and Samantha being able to be the mother figure, I felt that I was close to getting the judge to approve my request. The process took almost another year, but eventually, my wish came true. The court finally could see that I was a more fit parent and Mallory came to live with us while Joan had limited visitation rights. I was so happy to finally have my daughter back with me.

Some years later I became an electrician, working for a local electrical plant, and had gotten much more financially stable. Shortly after, Samantha and I bought a house with a big backyard in a nice suburban neighborhood, and everything was perfect. There was a Carvel ice cream shop down the street. Mallory and I would walk down there together. She loved Carvel. As the years passed, our house became a popular spot for block parties. Mallory had lots of neighborhood kids to hang out with during her school years. By the time she was in her early teens, Samantha and I were always holding some sort of party or neighborhood gathering at our house. She would help organize events and games with some of the other parents while I videotaped. I never realized during those times how important these memories would be to me later in life. Samantha and Mallory's relationship had started to become tense during the last couple of years. I could remember several arguments, but I stayed out of it most of the time because frankly I never totally understood the reasoning behind any of the disputes.

As I continued sipping my coffee, my thoughts fast-forwarded to a much later point in my life. I was 44, and Samantha and I were living in Asheville, North Carolina. We had decided to move away from New York several years before because we both felt it was getting vastly overpopulated and wanted a more laid-back lifestyle. We agreed that the North Carolina mountains would be our new home. It was so much more peaceful than the busy suburban lifestyle in Long Island. Mallory had moved out years before and gone to college. She and I rarely spoke because she and Samantha had gotten into a big clash. I remember the words from Samantha's mouth: "John, I don't want her in our life anymore. She's screwing things up between us."

"Samantha, love, she's my daughter. I know you two don't—" I was interrupted.

"Oh, John. Please, I can't deal with this." Samantha put her hands to her head.

"What's wrong? Are you okay?" I looked at her, concerned.

"My head, John. I get these bad headaches when I get upset. I just can't take it. Please, John. I feel dizzy. I just need to sit down."

I was terrified as I looked at her. I had seen her like this a few times before. For some reason, she had headaches when she got upset. We had seen a doctor together before, but they never could find anything wrong with her, which worried me even more.

"Samantha, don't worry. I'll make everything okay. I promise," I said, as I held her tightly in my arms. I decided not to argue the matter any further, fearing her sensitive condition.

I refocused my thoughts yet again to a different period. I was forty-nine and hadn't seen much of Samantha because I was so busy working. Times were hard. I had taken an immense cut in pay when we moved from New York to Asheville, North Carolina. The cost of living was cheaper down there, but the town was getting more crowded every year and jobs had become scarcer. I had been laid off from the first company I had been hired at in Asheville. After five years, they had to cut back on their expenses, and I found myself unemployed. I was able to get another job working for even less money and the hours were longer. A lot of wealthy retirees were moving into the area, which increased property values considerably, and that made it very hard for regular working-class people to afford new homes.

Samantha had been spending a lot of time with one of her friends, Jill, whom she had met through work about eight months before. They got along like sisters and spent an increasing amount of time together. I was just glad that she had someone to keep her company since I wasn't home much.

I was helping out with some construction on a job at the Grove Park Inn when I decided to come home early because I felt a little sick. When I pulled into the driveway, I saw both Samantha's and Jill's cars in the driveway. I figured they would have been at work. I walked in the front door, placing my flannel jacket and hat on the chair by the door. I heard music playing loudly upstairs.

"Hello? Samantha, I'm home," I called out. No answer. I climbed up the stairs toward the bedroom. The music grew louder as I approached the bedroom. It sounded like rock. The door was closed. I've never heard Samantha play music this loud before. Nothing could prepare me for what I was about to walk into.

Opening the door, I called out, "Samantha, I'm home—Jesus Christ! What the hell?" I couldn't believe my eyes. No. No. No. This couldn't be happening to me. I had no idea how to react as I saw Jill and Samantha lying naked in the bed fondling each other.

"Oh my God! John?" she said.

I suddenly felt lightheaded. I closed the door quickly, not wanting to see any more. I felt as if I were in a dream. Stunned, I slowly descended the stairs back to the front door. A moment later, Samantha came downstairs.

"John? John, wait," I could hear her calling my name, but her voice sounded so far away, drowned out by my thoughts. I picked up my hat and jacket, putting them both back on. Samantha grabbed my arm.

"John, please wait. Don't..." she pleaded.

"I...I just need some fresh air," I said. I felt like I had just jogged a marathon. I was out of breath, gasping heavily.

"Please, let me explain." She put her arm on my shoulder and I gently pushed it away.

"I just need some fresh air," I said again calmly.

"John, are you mad? John? Tell me what you're thinking, please. You're scaring me." I walked out the door, concentrating only on breathing as I got back in my truck and started to drive. I had no idea where I was going, just knew that I needed to drive. The next thing I remember, I was parked on the side of the road off the Blue Ridge Parkway just outside the entrance to Looking Glass Falls.

What did I do to deserve this? Is this what my life had been reduced to? Where did I screw up? I had been a good husband, hadn't I?

I got out of my truck and walked slowly down the narrow stepway leading toward the waterfall. There was no one else around that I could see. I saw the clear, pristine water spilling off the mountain. I had been down there many times before. It was my fortress of solitude when I needed to get away from everything. Every time I went there I admired the beautiful scenery, but that day none of that mattered to me. I walked for a long time, making my way up the trail near the top of the waterfall. When I reached the top, I thought about my childhood, all the major events that had happened in my life leading to this point. Mallory, Samantha, my parents, my brother, my friends.

"Where did I go wrong?" I screamed at the top of my lungs, my voice echoing throughout the wilderness. I felt lightheaded once again, slowly stumbling my way over to the stream, staring down at the flowing water. I started to cry. More than twenty years of marriage down the drain. And for what? I kneeled on some rocks, reaching my hand across the chasm to soak it, splashing some water in my face.

You could kill yourself right now, John. You could escape this hell. No, I can't do that, can I? I seriously considered the possibility. I could jump. I was pretty high up and if I jumped from the cliff, my neck should snap easily. I placed my feet right on the edge, staring at the bottom. I picked up one foot, reaching slightly forward. All I needed to do was lean one inch forward.

No! I stepped back, both feet secure on the ground once again. This isn't worth it. I owe myself more than that. I owe everyone else more than that. I'm getting outta this hell hole alright, but not this way. I walked back down the trail, reaching the step-way leading back to my truck parked on the side of the road. I threw my hat onto the seat and drove back to my house like a man on a mission.

I took quick, firm steps entering through the front door, slamming it hard behind me. Samantha suddenly appeared from the living room.

"Oh, John. I was so worried—"

"Shut the hell up!" I shouted.

"Just because I was with Jill doesn't mean I don't love you." Jill appeared from the kitchen, keeping her distance.

"What did I do wrong, Samantha? Huh? What? Everything I've done is for you! You said you wanted to move to North Carolina to get away, so we did! I knew I would take a huge pay cut, but I didn't care as long as we were both happy! I work these shit jobs with longer hours and less money for you! For Christ's sake, I gave up a relationship with my daughter for you! How could you? You bitch!" I was infuriated.

"Please, John. My head is starting to hurt. You know how I get when I get startled. Please, don't."

"Fuck you, Samantha! You know there's nothing wrong with you! Don't play that headache shit with me! Do you know the doctor told me once he believed you faked those headaches? Do you? I chose not to believe him when he said that. And the seizure you had a few years ago, he said the same thing about that. Even when I believed it was true, I told myself that I would take your side."

"John, please. Don't yell at her." Jill suddenly stepped forward from the hallway, butting into our argument.

"Jill, you stay outta this, or I swear to Christ..."

Jill stepped back.

"I'll get better. I promise. I won't ever do this again," Samantha wailed.

"I don't give a damn what you do anymore. I'm leaving you. You two have fun doing whatever it is the hell you do."

"John, no. Please don't. You can't."

"I'm leaving right now, Samantha." I turned around, heading back to the door. I stopped and turned back around. "Remember when you told me you wanted Mallory out of our life because she was in a lesbian relationship at the time? Well, it's pretty fucking ironic to find you here like this, huh?" I opened the door.

"Wait, what about your things? Aren't you going to take anything?" Samantha said.

"I've got the clothes on my back and my truck. I don't need anything else. You want the rest of this shit? The furniture, the appliances, the house—you can have it all! I don't give a fuck anymore!" I exited and slammed the door behind me.

I drove as far as Kingsport, Tennessee, parked my car at a La Quinta Inn, and decided to take the first flight to Seattle. The decision was spontaneous. I had always wanted to go to Washington state. I heard Seattle was beautiful except for the rain. Once there, I quickly found a temporary construction job and started a new life. I called Samantha a week later, and we agreed to file for divorce.

Suddenly I heard my cell phone ringing, which brought me back to the present. By the time I picked up, the signal was lost, and the call had been dropped. A minute later my phone beeped, indicating that whoever called had left a message. It was Bela. The recording quality was poor with a lot of static. I wasn't sure if my reception was bad or if her location was too remote.

"Det...Sandes. Th...Bela. I....curious. Rosie told me...she thinks...sa... your fri...was.... Is he...too? I wasn't sure...mention.... Hope that telling...okay?"

Damn. I had caller ID and tried to return her call but couldn't get through. I wondered what she wanted to tell me. A little while later I finished the rest of my coffee and got back into my car. Traffic was still heavy, but the extra dose of caffeine had given me a little pep, so I was able to tolerate it.

A half-hour later and I was back on West Dravus Street. I made sure to step sideways again so I could get through the claustrophobic corridor leading to the back entrance to the store. I opened the door and went into the waiting area with the same sign I had seen the first time:

Please Knock To Enter

I banged on the door, expecting a big thug to open the peephole slot and ask me what the hell I wanted. I waited. Silence. I banged again loudly. Nothing. Hmm. Seemed like nobody was home.

Who knows what the hell's going on around here? I wonder who lives in the apartment located in this building. Maybe they might be able to give me some more information on weirdo Frank. I walked around to the front of the building to what looked like the apartment suite. I could see a light on inside the window. A few cars were parked on the street in front of the building, so I guessed that somebody was home. I pushed the doorbell but didn't hear anything. I banged on the front door and waited. Silence. I gently turned the door handle. It was locked.

Hello?" I called from outside the house. "Anyone home? I'm a police detective." Although technically I wasn't a detective anymore, I still had my badge and pistol so I could say that I was without anyone knowing differently. I waited a minute but heard nothing. I started to walk back toward my car before I turned back around.

"The hell with it," I said. There was a small glass window in the middle of the front door. I eyeballed it carefully. I looked around the neighborhood to see if anyone was watching me. I saw no one. I took my coat off and held it in one hand. I then removed my pistol from my holster. Wrapping part of my coat around my firearm, I slammed the butt of my gun hard against the window. The glass broke, but the noise from the impact wasn't too loud. I reached inside the window and unlocked the door and opened it. I turned back around to make sure no one had seen me.

Slowly I approached the living room.

"Hello?"

No response. I walked slowly upstairs. Not a single person. It was a fairly large townhouse. When I reached the top of the stairs, I saw that there were three bedrooms and a small bathroom. I took a peek at each of the bedrooms. All the beds were empty and looked as if they hadn't been slept in at all. I looked in the bathroom as well and found nothing interesting. I went back downstairs, still trying to find any residents. The sofa was downstairs with a TV against the opposite wall. The refrigerator was in the kitchen downstairs with all of the normal stuff you would see in the normal places. Something odd suddenly occurred to me. I went back upstairs to peek inside the bedrooms. No clothes hung in any of the closets, nor were there any in the dresser drawers. No posters or pictures on the walls. I looked into the bathroom. Unused towels hung on rails. No open toothpaste or brushes lying around. I came back down the stairs into the living room. I looked around—no bookshelves or anything. It was almost like a hotel or something. Only the basic supplies were in view.

I opened the refrigerator. No food. Had the residents moved? I walked past the kitchen and saw a small door. It looked like it was a pantry of some sort. I turned the handle and was able to pull the door open a bit toward me. As I tried to pull, it jerked back and closed quickly like it was jammed or caught on something. I pulled harder and could see inside through the bottom of the door, but something was still caught toward the middle of the door. Shit! What the hell am I doing? It's just a damn pantry for God's sake. I started to walk away but then came back to the door. I was too curious now. I jerked it again with the same result. At this point, I was just too stubborn to give up. The hell with it. I grabbed the handle again and jerked it as hard as I could. *SNAP!* I heard the wood snap from behind the door. I opened the door and found to my surprise that small steps were leading to a lower-level room. This was no small pantry at all. I could see the large piece of wood that had broken off the door and picked it up, now understanding why the door would not open properly. There was a small latch lock attached to the backside of it. The cheap plywood door broke easily. How in the hell would someone have been able to lock this door? It would've had to have been locked from the other side since there was no keyhole. It was meant to keep people out, but why? I couldn't see anything down the stairs because it was pitch black. I tried to feel the wall to see if there was a light switch anywhere. When I couldn't find one, I started to walk down the steps very slowly and carefully. The last thing I wanted to do was fall and break my neck.

When I got to the bottom of the steps, I tried to feel my way around. I suddenly remembered that I had a small flashlight attached to my car keys. I turned it on and looked around. I saw a chair and an old sofa in one corner of the room. All of a sudden, I felt a sneezing sensation come on and let loose. *ACHOO!* My eyes were a little watery now.

I pulled a small cord hanging from the ceiling and a light came on. I could see that the room was extremely dusty, which explained my reaction. I rubbed my eyes, trying to adjust to all the dust. It looked like no one had been in here in a long time. Shelves along the wall held what mostly looked like junk. There was an old dial phone and books that probably had not been touched in years. A large wooden chest in another corner of the room, big enough to even… Please don't tell me there's a body in it. It did not have a lock on it so I tried to pry it open. It seemed to be jammed. Oh, shit. Here we go again. I had already broken the door. What the hell was I going to tell the people when they came home? For some reason, I didn't care. I don't know why. I tried the chest again, this time with more strength. It finally broke free. There were some cassette tapes of musicians that I had never heard of, a 1974 Volkswagen Beetle transmission manual, and a bunch of loose papers covered with even more dust. There was even a crowbar. I spent almost fifteen minutes looking around the room. At one point I thought I heard a voice in the room with me. I looked around carefully. I didn't see anyone lurking anywhere.

Maybe this is what it feels like to go senile. It probably didn't matter what rules I broke or how many houses I entered unlawfully because I'd just become some crazy old nut. I could always use that lame excuse as a last resort. I can just tell everyone my German shepherd tells me what to do. Wait, I don't have a German shepherd. Damn it. What's wrong with me? Concentrate here, John. After all this trouble, there's nothing here to give me a clue. I better get out of Dodge before…

There it was again. A voice. It sounded like a moan. The sound was very faint, but I was sure I heard it this time. I paused and remained perfectly still, holding my breath without realizing it. I heard it again. It was almost as if it was coming from another part of the building. I put my ear against one side of the wall and listened. Then I went to another side, and so on, trying to find the source of the sound. I heard it again. It was a very muffled moan and it sounded feminine. It seemed as if it was coming from somewhere below. How could that be? That was impossible. This was the ground floor and there was nothing beneath me. I looked around trying to see if maybe there was another door or something. I looked at the chest in the corner again, noting its massive size. By pure instinct, I proceeded to move it away from the wall with all the items inside. It was very heavy. I had to strain just to move it a few feet. I stared at it, amazed at what had been laid underneath.

Chapter 13

The chest had been placed directly over some sort of opening on the floor. It looked like a secret trap door, similar to the entrance to a storm cellar. I lifted the handle carefully and saw to my astonishment that this door led to a whole separate structure underneath the building. Distant noises sounded as if there were people down there. How strange. I descended the concrete stairs slowly and carefully. When total darkness prevented me from descending farther, I hesitated, considering whether or not to use my small flashlight. I turned it on and kept it close to my chest with one hand partially blocking the light so that it would not be seen easily, and cautiously moved down the stairs. I heard the voices getting louder. The closer I got to the bottom of the staircase; the more light was visible. The air had a much mustier smell now. I just hoped I didn't start sneezing again. When I finally reached the bottom, I no longer needed my flashlight, because this level was well lit. I peered around the corner, careful not to be seen. What I saw was a long hallway that looked to be about the length of a basketball court with several rooms on either side. I saw two men at the opposite end having a conversation. On the other end of the hallway where they stood, I saw another staircase that looked almost identical to the one I had just descended. I paused to listen to their conversation.

"How much longer you think these guys are gonna be, Earl?" said one of the men. He looked like a small man, but I could not tell for sure from so far away.

"Who knows? These pricks can go for hours sometimes. Whatever gets 'em off, I guess. I don't give a fuck, as long as I'm gettin' paid, Sam." This man Earl was much larger.

From one of the rooms, I heard a voice say, "Oh yeah, baby," followed by what sounded like a loud moan. Were people having sex in those rooms? What the hell was this, some kind of secret brothel? I continued to remain perfectly still, observing and listening to what was going on. I heard faint music coming from one of the rooms.

"Oh, fuck this. Let's go upstairs and get ourselves a beer," the man named Earl said.

"But what about them?" Sam replied, pointing toward the room.

"Don't worry so much, they'll be fine. We'll only be gone a few minutes."

Sam shrugged and followed Earl up the opposite staircase.

I remained still for another moment, listening to their footsteps get farther away as they ascended before I came out of my hiding place. The moaning got louder as I approached. Halfway down the hallway, I stopped in front of one of the doors. I could hear two people engaging in sexual activities within the room. A small glass window was located directly above each of the doors. Christ! What the hell am I doing here? I should call for backup. Too bad I left my cell phone in the car. The window was too high for me to see through. I looked around the large hallway for something I might be able to stand on. One of the men had been sitting on a metal folding chair by the stairwell on the other side. I hurried over and picked it up carefully and ran back to the door. I put the chair down and stood on it so I could peer through the glass into the room.

I saw a naked man standing with his back toward me and a woman kneeling on a large bed in front of him. Even though I couldn't see her face, I knew what she was doing. I was right; this place was an underground brothel. I looked around the room and saw a small mirror on one side and a night table right next to the bed. After a moment the woman got off the bed and stood up. I stared in horror at what I saw.

She was no woman. She was just a little girl. She couldn't have been more than ten years old. What in Christ's name? In a second, I had jumped off the chair and pulled my .38 out from its holster on my left hip. The door was unlocked and I wasted no time bursting in.

"Freeze! Police! You're under arrest! Get on the goddamn floor, you sick bastard!" I yelled at the repulsive pig. I was so enraged I could have shot him without any hesitation.

"Yo. Yo. Chill. All right," the pedophile replied, his hands up, scared shitless. I looked at him. He was a greasy, ratty-lookin' piece of shit. He had a medium build and I had no problem killing him right there if he decided to give me any trouble.

"On your stomach, hands behind your back, and shut the fuck up!" I roared.

He quickly got on the floor. Pulling out my handcuffs, I secured his hands behind him. I looked at the little girl.

"Are you alright?" I asked. She looked at me in total shock. She didn't say anything. I knelt beside her, keeping my gun pointed at the pedophile. I placed my hand on her shoulder. "Are you hurt?"

"N...no. Not any more than usual," she said to me, looking very confused.

"What?"

"A...are...are you a cop?"

"My name is Detective Sandes. What's your name, and how old are you?"

"Carrie. I'm nine."

"Carrie, are there any other girls your age down here?"

"I...I think I saw another girl who looked a year or two older than me go into that room across the hall." She pointed to another room.

"Quickly now, get dressed and come with me," I said. She did as I said and I grabbed her hand. "And you stay put!" I yelled at the cuffed man on the floor.

Just then the door across the hall opened, and a man with another young girl stepped out.

"What's all the screaming out here a—" He stopped abruptly when he saw me holding my gun aimed right at his head.

"Whoa...whoa... What's going on?" he said. His eyes darted a look at my gun.

"Get the fuck down! Now! You're under arrest!"

"Okay, okay." The man got on his stomach.

"It's okay, little girl. Come on, I'll get you out of here."

She did as I said while looking up at me, confused. "But I don't think the man was done yet," she said in a soft voice.

Jesus, how long has this been going on? I told Carrie to stay close to me and I grabbed the other girl's hand.

"What's your name and how old are you?" I asked her.

"Crystal. I'm eleven." At that instant, I heard the two men returning down the steps.

"What da fuck?" Earl yelled out.

"How'd he get down here?" Sam said.

"There's only one other way he coulda got down here, Sam."

"Freeze! Police!" I pointed my gun in their direction. I saw them both pull firearms from their inside coats. I pulled the trigger, blowing a hole in the shoulder of Sam the smaller man before he even had a chance to pull his weapon. He fell to the ground in agony. Earl fired back. I shuffled the girls as quickly as I could into one of the empty rooms. It was identical to the other room, with the same crappy bed, night table, and mirror.

"Do these rooms have locks?" I asked the girls.

"No, they don't," Crystal replied.

I took a quick peek outside the doorway. Earl fired a shot at me as soon as I popped my head outside. He had positioned himself in one of the rooms right next to the opposite stairwell, standing inside the doorway with his back against the jamb. Sam was nowhere in sight. I slammed the door shut again.

"How long have you two been involved in this? Where are your parents?"

"A couple of years ago this man named Frank picked me up in his van. He told me that my parents had died and that he would take care of me. He's been very good to me. He feeds me and gave me a place to stay," Carrie replied.

"I lived most of my life as an orphan. Frank adopted me when I was nine," Crystal said.

"Let me guess, his last name was Simone, right?"

She nodded yes.

"Christ! I can't believe this." I heard footsteps and more voices outside. I peeked out in the hallway again and saw Sam struggling back down the stairs with three more men who were armed and heading toward our room. Earl had moved one room closer and was almost directly across from us when he fired off three more shots. I ducked back inside to avoid getting hit. I quickly dropped to the floor and rolled onto my stomach to position myself just behind the doorway.

"Carrie, stay in that far corner over there away from the door. Crystal, I need you to get on the other side of the door. Reach and pull it open as fast as you can, but keep yourself low and behind the door so you don't get shot."

"Umm...okay." She was terrified.

"You'll be fine. I promise. Just do what I say. On a three count, okay? One...two...three!"

As Crystal swung the door open and jumped back, Earl fired, aiming for a headshot. But I was lying on my stomach, which gave me just enough time to get a clear shot right at his forehead. I took half a second to aim and squeezed. I blew a hole right through his forehead and his body hit the ground. I got back up and threw the door shut again. I could hear the other men shouting.

"Fuck! He shot Earl! Earl's dead!" one of the thugs yelled. Bullets flew through the door into the room. Three more men still stood outside, in addition to Sam. Carrie and Crystal crawled under the bed. Suddenly one of the goons kicked the door open and it flew off its hinges. Before the man could react, I raised my gun, unloading four shots directly into his chest. He screamed in terror before slumping to the floor. Blood spurted everywhere. The door lay on the floor blown apart. Now the three of us had no cover. Sam was just inside the stairwell, pointing his gun, and the other two men had disappeared. Just then a bullet came through the wall right above the bed. Carrie and Crystal both quickly rolled out from under the bed. I grabbed the girls and pulled them toward the opposite wall. I felt another bullet whiz by the left side of my head. Goddammit! The bastards were right next to us.

I stuck my hand outside the doorway and pointed it into the room to my left without looking, firing away hoping to get a lucky shot at the bastard. I unleashed some more rounds into the room to my right. More bullets came through the walls. The girls were now against the wall directly opposite where the door had been. The firing had ceased and I could hear them trying to reload. I remembered the mirror. I quickly picked it up, breaking it with the butt of my gun, and grabbed a shard of mirror glass. Out of bullets, I reloaded with the spare magazine that I always carried. I squatted by the doorway and held the shard out in the hall so I could see where the shooter was in the room to my left. I could see his beady little eyes staring into the mirror. At that instant I positioned my gun, carefully aiming in the opposite direction, and unloaded.

"Aaah!" I heard him scream, I dived into the room, firing wildly.

"He's dead, Jim," I said sarcastically, imitating the character of Dr. McCoy from Star Trek. My awkward sense of humor helped me get through tough situations like this when I needed it.

I wheeled around, went back into the hallway, and kicked in the door to the room where the other man remained. He fired his gun at me, but the bullet went wide, just missing my shoulder. I fired back and blew a hole through his throat.

I quickly remembered Sam. Where the hell did he go? I didn't see him or the two pedophile scumbags. They must have bailed while I was getting trigger happy. It had been a few years since I'd had to kill someone. But I'd just killed four men and didn't give a shit. I had to protect these children.

I told the girls to follow closely behind me as I ascended the stairwell opposite from where the men had entered. I could guess where this led. When I reached the top, I found myself in what appeared to be a large room with a big conference table and wooden chairs. I saw a door on the other end of the room. I motioned to the girls to remain back as I readied my gun. I quickly opened the door, expecting gunfire. Nothing. I looked through the doorway and saw a room with a steel-barred window. Wait a minute. Of course. I quickly rushed to the window, remaining alert for any more shooters. As I came through, I found myself in a familiar room where I had been days earlier. I looked at the wall directly above the bars to read the sign: **Erotica Fliks Open 24/7**

That hallway downstairs was the gateway between the store and the apartment. I guessed the apartment was owned by Frank as well.

"Carrie? Crystal? Are you two still back there?" I called back toward the room at the top of the stairs. They slowly came out.

"Follow me." I saw that the entrance doorway was now wide open. I proceeded outside toward the narrow corridor, watching for any shooters. Finally, I came around the front of the house. I pointed to my car down the street.

"You two see that car? We're going to run for it. Stay low and follow behind me. Go now!" We ran and got in. Nobody fired at us. I guess Sam and whoever else was upstairs were long gone. I quickly started the car and drove away.

I reached inside my glove compartment to grab my cell phone and called Larry.

"Hello?"

"Larry. It's John."

"John, what's going on?"

"I'm in trouble and I need help."

Chapter 14

I explained to Larry everything that had happened under the storefront and all the events that had taken place since. I even detailed to him my conversations with Lauren regarding Rodriguez's disappearance. I had not intended to tell him all this so soon but felt that the urgency of my current situation required me to do so. I told him that I was going to take the two girls down to the police station and call for backup to have the place searched. He told me not to bother, that he would send a team down right away. He warned me to stay away from the crime scene. He stated that the fact that I had committed unlawful entry might make things a little difficult. He also reminded me that I had again failed to follow orders and was supposed to be on leave. Nevertheless, he didn't sound upset and said he would handle everything and for me to just get the girls to the station.

While driving back downtown, I had constantly been looking through my rearview mirror to see if any of the thugs had been following us. I didn't see anyone. When I arrived at the police station, I brought the girls into one of the waiting areas. At this point, I was just relieved and thankful I was able to get the girls to safety. My cell phone rang. It was Larry. I told the girls to stay put while I walked down the hall to answer.

"Yeah, Larry."

"John, are you at the station yet?"

"Yeah, I just got here. The girls are in the waiting area. I was just about to report what happened to the desk officer."

"Don't bother. I'm sending another detective down there right now. I need you to come over to my house as quickly as possible. I've got something I need to discuss with you regarding this case. I've got some information we could use."

"Well, can't you tell me now?"

"No, I have to show you. Please, just try and get here as soon as you can."

"Okay, Larry. I'll be there soon."

I walked over to the front desk and asked the female officer who was sitting there to watch the two girls in the waiting area across the hall, informing her that another detective would be there soon to speak with them. I went back to the waiting area and assured the girls that everything would be okay, informing them if they needed anything in the meantime not to hesitate to ask the nice female officer across the hall. I knew they were in good hands.

I left the police station and arrived at Larry's house within twenty minutes. He lived in a very nice upper-class housing development. It was a gated community that had a security officer on guard 24/7. When I approached the front entrance, the man came out of the booth toward my car.

"Sir, I'm here to see Larry Wegmueller."

"What's the address?"

"613 Rombergh Court."

"Hold just one minute." The guard went back inside the booth. I waited impatiently. After a minute he came back carrying a clipboard.

"I just need you to sign in, sir," he said.

After I gave him my signature, he opened the gate and waved me through. I made a few turns and pulled up in front of his house. I approached the front door and rang the doorbell. A minute later, Larry answered the door. He was wearing a black t-shirt with jeans. His hair was soaking wet.

"Good to see you, John. Please excuse me—I jumped into the shower right after I called you."

Larry went to the kitchen, grabbed a coffee mug from a cabinet, and prepared some coffee.

"Would you like some?"

"No, thank you. What is it you wanted to show me?"

"Hold on just one minute and follow me upstairs into my study. We'll talk there."

I followed Larry upstairs into the study. There was a big desk in the middle of the room with a computer resting on one side and a printer/fax machine on the other and two big leather armchairs seated opposite one another. There were also two large bookcases on either side of the walls. They were filled with law enforcement–related books: *Black's Law Dictionary*, *Bennet's Guide to Crime Scene Investigation Vol. 26.*, *Advanced Criminal Forensics*, *Policies of Criminal Investigations*.

"Larry did the team arrive—"

My cell phone went off again. I could tell from the number that it was Bela calling. I had forgotten to call her back.

"I'm sorry, Larry. Just let me get this real quick."

Larry waved his hand in the air, gesturing for me to go ahead.

"Bela, I'm sorry I didn't get back to you. I'm in the middle of something extremely important. Can I call—" I was quickly interrupted.

"Detective, I just wanted make sure you got my message 'bout you friend."

"I got it but it was hard to understand with all the static."

"I called to you so I tell you that he in the hotel that night. Rosie recognize him."

"Wait. Huh?"

"That man you talking to earlier. Rosie saw him. He in the hotel night man get murdered."

"What? That's impossible. Are you sure?"

"Yes, Detective. She no remember at first who he was, but then later she remember." My body froze. My heart was beating rapidly.

"I need to call you back." I quickly ended the call without giving her a chance to say any more. Larry looked at me suspiciously. There was a moment of silence.

"What was that about, John?"

"N...nothing important," I said, trying not to sound too shaken up. Suddenly I remembered something. I looked at his fax machine.

"Uh, Larry, can I use your fax quick? I need to send something."

"It's all yours, John," he said calmly, staring at me.

I walked around to the side of the desk where the fax machine was placed and took out the photo I had found in Randy Limehouse's New York apartment. I unfolded it, pretending as if I was going to fax it to someone. I laid the sheet along with the feeder tray and looked at the fax number at the bottom:

Sent by 555-786-0098

I looked at Larry's fax machine display screen:

Your number is: 555-786-0098

What Bela told me was true. I was still trying to make sense of it all when I heard myself blurt out, "Larry, what is your connection with Randy Limehouse?" I looked back at him, holding up the piece of paper.

"What are you talking about, John?"

I realized then that in speaking out I'd lost whatever opportunity I had to learn the truth without revealing what I knew. I had no choice but to confront Larry directly. Maybe there was a logical explanation.

"Larry, did you know Randy Limehouse personally?"

"No, I've never met him."

"But you sent this fax to him with Phillip Rodriguez's address information. Why?"

"Oh, John, come on. What is that paper you're holding? That's preposterous."

"Rosie said she saw you in the hotel the night that Limehouse was murdered!" I had begun to speak impulsively, without thinking. I had to know what the hell was going on.

"Give me a break. I've never seen that girl in my life," Larry said rather unconvincingly.

"Well, I found this piece of paper in his condo when I went to New York. Yes, I searched through his residence. You faxed this to him. Your fax number matches the one this piece of paper was sent from. What the hell is going on here?"

"Now, John, relax. Let me explain."

"Larry, did you have something to do with his murder?" I asked in disbelief. I hated to openly accuse Larry, but I had to.

Larry looked me in the eye before picking up his mug and finishing his coffee. "I know what goes on below Erotica Fliks. I've known for quite some time. Frank has clients who pay top dollar for some of those children." His calmness was frightening.

"But, what does that have to do with all—"

"What does it have to do with all this? You see, John, Frank hands over a percentage of what he charges, and I put some of that toward funding for the department and, of course, a nice little cut for me. Who cares about what happens to a few unknown children here and there? Frank's funding is one of the reasons why we have one of the best police departments in the nation. As long as they keep it quiet and the press doesn't find out, what difference does it make? Do you have any idea how much money I get from them? I'm talking numbers in the millions."

"John, I hate to do this. I would offer you some money to keep quiet, but I know you're not the type to accept bribes. Put your hands up," he suddenly pulled out his gun and aimed it at my face. This couldn't be Larry.

He stood up from his chair. "I honestly didn't think that you would get this far. I know you've had your days, but your investigation methods are flawed."

I pulled my cell phone out of my pocket and began to dial the police station, but I quickly froze.

"Forget it, John. Just think about everything for a moment. I won't hesitate to blow your head off. I know how to make it look like an accident. I'll tell them you went nuts. Everyone would believe me. It's easy to see that you haven't been too mentally stable lately. Don't you see that I was only looking out for the greater good of the community? We're talking about a few unknown kids here and there, nothing more. If it weren't for the things I've done, you wouldn't have been able to capture some of the criminals you've caught during your career. You should be thanking me." After a brief pause, he added, "ol' man." He smiled at me, but it was evil and twisted.

Had I worked for this man all those years? I had been taken as a fool. I couldn't let him get away with this.

At that instant, I lunged forward, knocking him over the desk. I reached for my gun. He knocked it away, and it skittered under his desk. He was on top of me with his hands squeezed tightly around my neck. I pushed him off, freeing myself of his chokehold. I managed to stand up, but he jumped on my back, trying to bring me back down. I spun out of the room and threw us both tumbling headlong down the stairs, spilling onto his living room floor. I quickly got up. My knees had taken a hard impact from the fall and were aching badly.

"Let's see what you got, ol' man." His punch nailed me right in the gut. He then grabbed the back of my head, smashing my face into a hallway mirror. My face was cut, blood oozing, but I managed to stay on my feet. He swung at my head again, narrowly missing and giving me just enough time to pop him in the right side of his ribs. He stumbled, and I gave him a clean left hook to the nose. Blood trickled down one of his nostrils. I turned around quickly to retrieve my gun, only to see Frank Simone standing right behind me with a small baton. *Bam!* For an instant, I felt the hard steel tip connect with the side of the head. Then nothing....

Chapter 15

It was a cool breezy summer Sunday evening in late August 1967. I was riding happily in my '57 cherry-red Corvette. I had the top down and was enjoying the wind blowing in my face while I held a cigarette in one hand. I had purchased the car just a little over a year ago. I was a far cry from being rich, but I had saved up enough money during the last few years. I wasn't sure if I could keep it too much longer because I would need some extra cash to put a down payment on this house that I was looking at. Despite all the drama, I was in a pretty good mood. I was twenty-seven years old, and my world was far from perfect. But I couldn't complain too much. Joan and I had just gotten divorced. We had a one-year-old daughter, Mallory. Our marriage had been destined for disaster from the very beginning, turning into two years of hell. We made the mutual decision to end it. Joan had started seeing another man within a couple of weeks of the divorce. I was just happy to be free of it all. The only thing that upset me was Mallory. Joan ended up having custody of Mallory, while I had visitation rights. I knew in my heart that I was the more responsible and better parent, but the judge felt a child that young belonged with her mother.

I turned the AM radio to my favorite jazz music station. There's nothing like driving to jazz. I was on my way to the Liberty Bowling Alley. It was in Queens, just a short drive from where I lived in Brooklyn. I was meeting my friend Anthony to get a few games in. Bowling was the hippest thing to do these days. I found Anthony waiting inside.

"Hi, Johnny. Are you ready to get creamed tonight?" He chuckled at me.

"In your dreams, pal. I'll show you the 'Sandes Strikeball,'" I joshed back at him.

We went to the concession stand and got ourselves some burgers, fries, and soda to enjoy while we bowled. An hour went by, and we had bowled three games. I won two of the three. I was standing, joking around with Anthony. He gave me a nudge.

"Hey, Johnny, check out that group of girls."

Four girls about our age had walked in, but there was one in particular who grabbed my attention. She was beautiful—tall and slender with long blond curly hair. I saw the girls approach one of the lanes. I decided to walk over and talk to her.

"Go get her, pal," Anthony cheered me on.

I casually walked over to her, trying to appear as calm and cool as possible. The truth was that I was nervous as hell.

"You ladies like to bowl, huh?"

One of the girls, a brunette, looked over at me. *"Golly gee, girls, we got a real Einstein here,"* *she mocked me, giggling along with the rest of the girls.*

I brushed off the cynical remark. *"Oh, yeah? Well, guess what? I can bowl a 220."*

Even though I was talking to all four of them, I was looking directly at the blonde that had caught my eye.

"Wow, you must practice a lot," *she said with a smile.*

"Would you mind if my friend and I bowled with you ladies? I can give you some tips," I said, pointing across the room at Anthony.

"Sure, whatever," the brunette said trying to brush him off while the other girls smiled.

I motioned for Anthony to come over.

"I'm Johnny, and this is Anthony."

"I'm Wanda," the sarcastic brunette said. "That's Sheila," she pointed at a redhead.

"I'm Wendy." The other brunette quickly interrupted Wanda and smiled.

I paid little attention to the other three girls, still staring at the other lovely blonde.

"My name is Samantha," she said to me. She had the most gorgeous blue eyes.

"Samantha, would you mind if I threw the first ball, so I can show you the proper way?"

"Sure, go ahead," she said.

Stepping up to the lane, I threw the ball and knocked nine pins down on the first roll. With the second roll, I knocked down the remaining pin for an easy spare. I could see Anthony doing his best to flirt with the other girls. Sheila and Wendy were laughing hysterically at his jokes, while Wanda looked as if she was somewhat intrigued but trying to appear unimpressed.

"Okay, now you try. Let me go get you a ball. What weight do you use?"

She giggled at me. "No, thank you. I've got my own." She reached down underneath one of the chairs and pulled out a tan bowling bag with a bright pink ten-pound ball. I stared as she held the ball, swung her arm back, and rolled it. Her leg position was perfect. CRASH! All ten pins fell. She made it look effortless. Wow. I couldn't believe it.

"How often do you bowl?" I asked her with a shocked look.

"I bowled in leagues all through high school," she said, chuckling.

In the first game, Samantha bowled a 235. I had a mediocre 180. Anthony scored a 155, just barely beating out the other three girls. Wendy was right behind him with a 152. By that time, Anthony had his arm wrapped around Wanda's shoulder. I guess they had hit it off. The two of them decided they didn't want to bowl anymore and went to the concession stand to get some more drinks. I bowled another game with Samantha, Sheila, and Wendy. This time Samantha bowled a 252.

"Wow, I've never seen a girl bowl that well before."

"Oh, that was nothing. My average is 270. I bowled a 300 once, too."

Here I was trying to brag about my pitiful athletic skills. I was slightly embarrassed, but I still had fun. Wanda and Anthony came back over.

"Oh, I think we should go now. We've been here a while. Shall we head off, girls?" Wanda said.

"Yeah, I'm beat," Wendy replied.

"Well, it was very nice to meet you, Johnny. It was swell," Samantha said to me. The other girls waved bye, while Anthony and Wanda exchanged phone numbers. As Samantha started to walk away, I ran back to her.

"Samantha, would you be interested in going out with me sometime?" I asked.

"Uh, sure. Let me give you my number." She grabbed a napkin and pen from the concession stand, wrote it down, and handed it to me. She left with her friends after giving me a quick smile and wave.

Anthony nudged me in the side. "Man, that Wanda sure is a fox. I'm gonna ask her to the drive-in on Friday. That new James Bond flick is playing. I think the title is You Only Live Twice." Anthony was hyped up now. "What about you, Johnny? Are you gonna call Samantha? She's a real looker, and on top of that, she can bowl. What more can you ask for?"

I looked at him and smiled. I didn't need him to tell me what to do. Of course, I'd call her.

I thought about Samantha during the next few days. I had called her on Wednesday, asking her if she wanted to go out into the city on Friday to the Golden Horn dance club on Broadway Street. They played a mix of '50s, modern tunes, and sometimes swing music. She had told me on the phone she loved to dance. I told her I did too. In reality, though, I had no idea how to dance. Hopefully, I could manage some moves without looking too awkward.

So tonight was the big night. It was 6:45 p.m., and I had just gotten back home after visiting with Mallory at Joan's. Mallory was *speaking now; she was extremely smart for her age. I missed not having her around all the time. I tried not to worry about it too much, but it was hard.*

Tonight, however, was going to be grand. I was supposed to pick up Samantha at 8:00 p.m. I took a cold shower and then gave myself a nice, fresh shave. I threw my best dress clothes onto the ironing board, pressing them to perfection. I wore a white collared shirt with a striped tie and khaki dress pants with a navy-blue blazer. I put a small amount of gel in my hair and combed it straight back to give myself a spruced-up look. I jumped into my Corvette. I must have spent at least ten minutes procrastinating, asking myself whether to have the top up or down, before I finally drove off. What would Samantha prefer? I decided to leave it down. I was betting she'd think my convertible was cool.

I pulled into her driveway at 8:00 p.m. sharp. She lived in a rather wealthy neighborhood. The house was huge. I rang the doorbell, and a girl who appeared to be six or seven years older than Samantha answered.

"Can I help you?" she said to me.

"Yes, I'm here to pick up Samantha."

"Who are you?" She gave me a funny look.

"My name is Johnny Sandes."

She turned around and yelled into the house, "Samantha, there's a guy here to see you!" I expected the girl to at least invite me inside, but she didn't.

I heard Samantha yell down from upstairs, "Tell him I'll be right there."

"Sam's still putting her girdle on." *The girl laughed.*

"Elise, that's not funny."

Samantha finally came running down the stairs. She looked stunning. She was wearing a red blouse and a white skirt with matching high-heeled shoes.

Everything about her was attractive: her eyes, her curly blond hair, her long legs.

"Do mom and dad know you're going out with him? He looks like a strange one," *the other girl joked rather crudely.*

"Yes, Elise, now go away," *Samantha said as she pulled the door shut behind her.*

The two of us walked to my car. I opened the door for her and walked hurriedly around and got into the driver's seat.

"I'm sorry, Johnny. That was my sister back there. She can be a real pain sometimes. I have two other sisters, but she's the most difficult. She should have at least invited you in."

"Hey, no big deal. We all deal with those things. My brother, Billy, and I used to have our differences." *I shrugged it off, excited that we were in the car, headed out into the night.*

"So, do you still live with your family?"

"Nah, I'm living in an apartment in Brooklyn, not too far from here. My mother lives nearby. My brother is living in the city; he's learning how to make guitars. He's doing an apprenticeship, studying under a guy named John D'Angelico. Ever heard of him?"

"Wow, that's pretty neat. I've heard of that guy. People say he's one of the greatest guitar makers."

"Yeah, it's pretty swell." I smiled at her.

We arrived at The Golden Horn, and I paid our entry fee. The floor was packed with people moving to "Breaking Up Is Hard to Do" by Neil Sedaka. We found a booth and sat for a few minutes. I ordered a scotch on the rocks, while she sipped some merlot. The next song that came on was "Tutti Frutti" by Little Richard, and that one got the crowd wild. I asked Samantha to dance, leading her to the floor. She started shaking her body to the rhythm of the beat without a care in the world. I was nervous but didn't let on. I did the twist for a few minutes since it was one of the few moves I did know. As the night wore on, the music changed to more current songs, playing tunes like "I'm a Believer" by The Monkees and "Strangers in the Night" by Frank Sinatra. The last song of the night was the '50s tune "Earth Angel" by The Penguins. It was a slow song, and I held Samantha close. I could smell the scent of her hair as she leaned on my shoulder. I wished this moment could last forever.

It was 1 a.m. when we left. Music was still playing, but not many people were dancing. As I drove Samantha home, we talked about which musicians we liked and what songs we enjoyed the most. I pulled into her driveway and parked.

"I had a really good time tonight, Johnny," she said, smiling at me.

"It was fun. I enjoyed being with you."

"Well, thanks again. Give me a call sometime."

"Okay, definitely," I said. We stared into each other's eyes for a moment. She started to reach for the door handle. My heart was beating rapidly, and I didn't know if I had the guts to make a move. Would she want me to? I wondered. Suddenly I grabbed her hand before she could open the door.

"Samantha."

"Y...Yes."

I leaned over and kissed her right on the lips, unsure of her reaction. She put her arm on my chest and leaned closer. We embraced, and I knew I was in love. Suddenly everything started to fade. What's happening? Samantha, where are you? Everything disappeared into blackness....

Chapter 16

My head felt awful. I opened my eyes, but I couldn't see a thing.

"Samantha? Samantha?" I called out.

I finally realized it was all a dream, some images dredged up from the past. I knew I was awake but still couldn't see anything. It took me a moment to adjust to my position. I was lying on my side with my arms handcuffed behind my back. As I tried to sit up, my head struck something. I was in agony. My head throbbed. Where was I? I tried to gather my thoughts for a few minutes. The pain was unbearable. Wait a minute! I'm moving. I'm in the trunk of a car. After what seemed like an eternity, the car stopped. I heard doors being opened. Someone walking on gravel. Keys clanging. The trunk opened, and Larry was peering at me.

He pulled me out and threw me onto the ground. Frank Simone stood next to him. From what I could see, we were out in the country—lots of trees, some grassy hills, a lake in the distance, and farther away—a snow-capped mountain. The sky was dark. I wondered how long I had been out. I couldn't tell exactly what time it was, but judging from our location and the minimum time it would have taken to get here, it was probably close to two or three o'clock in the morning.

"What the hell have you done, Larry? You killed all those people. Leo Johnson, Randy Limehouse, K.C. Wingate!" I said.

"K.C. Wingate? No, John. I didn't kill K.C. Wingate. I would have hoped you thought more of me than that."

"What? What do you mean, you…?" I couldn't think straight, thanks to the friendly whack on the head Frank gave me.

"John, don't you realize? You found the evidence yourself. K.C.'s hairs on Johnson's body. The sperm was found on the girl's body. Leo Johnson killed K.C. Wingate after he raped her."

"And you killed Leo Johnson?"

"You're damn right I did. You see, good ol' Leo was a partner of Frank's. The two of them ran the operation. He was charging top dollar for the girls he and Frank were bringing in. But he started to get out of control. Unfortunately, he had a real kiddie porn fetish himself, which is what did him in. Pretty soon he started stalking some of the children in various elementary schools throughout the area. One day while he was taking pictures, he saw K.C. walking out of her school. He watched her for several days before he finally abducted her."

"Why didn't I find any more of her DNA in Johnson's apartment suggesting that he raped her?"

"You wouldn't. Not in his apartment. Johnson brought K.C. down to Erotica Fliks that night. Frank wasn't there when Johnson brought her in. He took the girl down to one of the rooms and had his way with her. The girl fought pretty hard, kicking and screaming wildly. Johnson tried to quiet her but ended up strangling her in the process. He called Frank later that evening and explained what happened. Frank told me then. Of course, I couldn't allow this maniac to run around, especially not in my district. I have a reputation to maintain."

"So, then you killed Johnson and hid K.C.'s body."

Larry laughed loudly. "Wrong again, Sherlock. I made the bastard do it himself. I told him that if he did it, I could keep things quiet. He told me that he used to live in Vancouver and knew of a storage complex where he could hide the body. I told him to go ahead and get rid of it. Hell, I knew eventually someone would find it, but nothing would connect it to me so I didn't care. It's funny. I never imagined you would find the damn thing. I found it very interesting when you asked me for permission to go to Vancouver. Even then I didn't think you would find it; but when you called me the night that you did, I was stunned. I mean, no offense, John. You're a good detective, but not that good."

"So, you made Johnson dispose of the body himself before you shot him."

"Now you're getting somewhere, ol' man. You see, there was one witness who said she got a pretty good look at Leo Johnson. Leo Johnson had been busted once before for having sex with a minor, and his profile was on file."

"There was no such reference in the system. I checked."

"I'm sure you did, John, but not before I had it erased." I thought for a moment about what Larry had just said. Suddenly I realized.

"Rodriguez knew, didn't he? He knew because he was the senior engineer who audited all the changes to the database. He saw that Johnson had been deleted from the system. You bastard!" I said.

"It had to be done, John. He approached his manager to tell him what I'd done. But everyone knows that I have all the power in this organization. I told his manager it was just a minor misunderstanding. I tracked Phillip down one day and told him not to tell anyone. I told him he would have to quit his job and say it was voluntary. I told him if he didn't, I'd have him killed. He was scared shitless and promised to keep his mouth shut. He gave his notice on a Monday but was going to work the rest of the week. I kept my eye on him. He was acting erratic, and I didn't trust him to stay quiet for too long."

"And Randy Limehouse?"

"He was just some thug I hired to get rid of Phillip Rodriguez."

"So, once again you got someone else to do your dirty work for you before having them killed."

"Bingo. Limehouse intercepted Rodriguez at a gas station in an isolated spot off the highway. It's no coincidence that the police haven't found his car yet," he said, smiling proudly.

"Where's the body?"

"I've disposed of it. You don't need to worry about that."

"How come no one heard any gunshots after Limehouse and Johnson were shot?" I asked.

"Oh, that's simple. Because of this," Larry pulled out a long, thin metal object. I looked at it closely and realized it was a silencer. "These things are easy for someone like me to get a hold of," he laughs.

"One more question."

"Ask away."

"What was the deal with the apartment building and Erotica Fliks?"

"When Frank bought that space several years ago, he thought it was strange at first too. Originally some people owned that unit, but when they had decided to move Frank bought the home from them. He knew just how to put that additional space to use. He was charging those rooms by the hour and had other girls working that house. Not children, just an average whorehouse with legal-age girls to make some money. Frank stopped using the older girls when he realized that the key to making big bucks is with children. You'd be amazed at the people who come flocking for this type of thing. I think it's some sick shit, but the money is good."

Frank could stand it no longer. "Enough of this small-talk bullshit, Larry!" he yelled.

"Calm down, Frank," Larry snapped back at him.

I assessed my surroundings again. "So, where the hell are we?" I asked.

"This is some private property I own. We're about ten miles from the border of the North Cascades, Washington National Park. Way in the distance over there is Mount Shuksan. Isn't she a beauty?" He pointed to the enormous peak.

I said nothing, feeling disgusted. A moment later a green Jeep Cherokee pulled up next to Larry's car. The driver looked familiar, but I couldn't place him. A moment later, I was shocked to see Carrie and Crystal in the back. They both looked panicked.

"What are they doing here? I dropped them off at the police station. How did you—"

"Oh, John. I don't believe you've met my friend here. This is Emerson Locke." I looked at him more closely. Locke was a tall, fit man with light brown hair and a mustache. He reached for a cowboy hat from the inside of his car and put it on. Now I remembered that I had seen him the other day walking into Larry's office building. I think I may have seen him a few other times walking around in the precinct, but never thought much about it. He opened up the trunk and pulled out a shotgun. He held it in one hand, keeping his eye on me.

Larry said, "I make sure that Emerson here stays very low-key. We're old friends. Known you what now? About twenty-one, twenty-two years?"

"Somethin' like that," Locke replied.

I didn't like this guy. I had a real bad feeling about him. He had a deep, raspy voice and appeared to be a little younger than Larry. He was wearing jeans and brown worker boots with that off-white cowboy hat I had seen before. He looked like the Marlboro man. I sensed that he was the kind of guy who just wanted to hurt somebody.

"I use him when I need to cut a few corners," Larry explained.

"What are you going to do to me, Larry?" I was more awake now, and my anger was slowly returning.

"Well, John, I would have liked to have kept you around a little longer, but somehow I just knew that you wouldn't see things my way. I don't think you understand that sometimes you have to make a few sacrifices here and there for the greater good of the community. That's what I did here."

"You gonna kill the girls too, you son of a bitch?" I retorted.

"Now, I don't see any need for that. Frank's arranged for them to be packed off. To the Philippines, I believe, is that right, Frank?"

Frank nodded his head yes.

"Frank has clients all over who will pay good money for girls like these, and besides, these two aren't exactly innocent anymore. You girls have been doing it for years now, right?" Larry sneered at them.

"How can you do this?" I started to stand up, but Locke gave me a hard kick right in the stomach with his boot. I fell back on the ground, coughing.

"Frank, Emerson, take the girls to my cabin. Frank, call your clients and give them directions so they can pick up those two tomorrow. The sooner we get rid of them, the better." Frank and Marlboro Man put the girls back in the Jeep and drove off.

"I'm sorry, John. I just can't take the risk with you. Come on, the two of us are going for a nice little hike," he said, pulling me to my feet.

"Where are we going?"

"Oh, you'll find out soon enough."

We started walking up the hills. I had no idea where he was taking me.

We must have walked almost a mile before we came to a field, in the middle of which stood a large shed resembling a barn.

"John, how do you like this fine piece of property I have here? It's a great place to hunt, and there isn't a damn person around for miles." He laughed hysterically. I had no idea that Larry was this crazy. Not in all the years, I'd known him.

"You see that cabin up there? I built it myself twenty years ago. I worked on it off and on for a whole year."

We approached the shed, and he opened the set of doors. It was much bigger than it looked from the distance. I estimated the structure to be almost three stories high. There were numerous types of equipment and tools lying around, including handsaws, hammers, and hatchets, as well as an array of power tools. Bales of hay were stacked up against the sides of the walls, and ladders lead to various lofts in the structure. A big swimming pool–shaped metal container stood toward the back of the building.

"The person who used to own this was a horse breeder, and before it was a brewery, which is why some of this equipment is here," Larry said, pointing at the objects. "As you'll find out, a lot of this stuff still can be of use to me. I've had a special formula prepared just for tonight's event." Larry sneered as he pulled me toward the back so I could peer inside the giant container. "You see that clear liquid in this big container? I'll tell you right now, it's not water." Larry paused a moment, staring into my eyes.

"Hydrochloric acid. I'm sorry if this seems a bit clichéd, John. The truth, though, is the stuff works. I don't give a shit about being fancy or having some over-the-top puzzle that you have to solve to escape. When your body dissolves in the acid, it will be almost impossible for anyone to ever know that your body was disposed of here. Of course, all this work is just an extra precaution. I don't believe anyone will ever even think to look for you up here anyway."

"So that's it, huh? You're just gonna throw me in there?"

"No, John. Honestly, I couldn't bear to see you suffer that way. I don't have the stomach to watch your body dissolve while you scream. I'll just shoot you first and throw your body in there to destroy the evidence." Larry pulled out his gun and aimed it at my head.

"I'm sorry it had to end this way."

Chapter 17

How the hell was I gonna get out of this? It sure seemed like the end. There was nothing else I could do.

Larry looked into my eyes, "turn around, John."

I did as he said. Is this the way I'm gonna go out? No, not yet. I'll be damned if I'll die quietly. I swung my body backward, startling Larry, and kicked him in the groin. As he keeled over, I kicked again even harder, this time connecting squarely with the side of his head. He fell over. I couldn't believe it—I knocked the big ox out. There was no telling when he would wake up, though. I just hoped to God that he had what I needed. I squatted down on the ground, with my hands behind me trying to feel inside Larry's pockets. Yes! He had the keys in his pocket. I managed to grab them, and after fumbling for a moment, I unlocked the cuffs. My arms were finally free. I placed the cuffs in my front pocket and I picked up his gun off the floor, putting it inside my holster. I hurried outside, trying to collect myself and figure out what I needed to do. I was still groggy and exhausted. I had walked maybe a hundred feet from the shed before I felt tackled from behind and thrown hard against the ground.

"You got a lucky shot in back there. Did you think it was gonna be that easy, ol' man?"

Larry was on top of me with his knee in my back. He jabbed me in the back of the head.

"You can't outfight me, John. You're not strong enough."

Larry probably had at least fifty pounds on me. I fidgeted around for a moment before finally shaking him off. I rolled and quickly stood up, but not before he nailed me with a right punch to my face. I quickly retaliated with a left jab. He was too close for me to pull the gun. I swung another jab and missed. Larry grabbed me around the waist, putting me in a bear hug, throwing my body back onto the ground. He landed on me again, reaching for the gun. I seized his hand and the two of us struggled for control. I pulled up a clump of grass and dirt with my free hand and shoved it into his eyes, making him loosen his grip. I jerked the gun away and hurled it as far as I could while lying on my back. It landed about thirty yards away.

Now it was just the two of us in this field with nothing nearby except the shed and the rest of the wilderness. I popped him in the cheek and rolled over on top of him, seizing the opportunity to attempt to stand. As soon as I got up, Larry clutched my head, jabbing his fingers in my eyes. I flipped him over my back, sending him down onto the ground with a thud and knocking the wind out of him. He got back up, keeping a short distance between us. He paced back and forth, glaring at me.

"You've been very lucky so far. You ready for round two?" he said.

"Bring it on, asshole."

He didn't charge me this time. He held both hands in front. I prepared for the biggest fight of my life.

"You won't outbox me either, John," he said with a sinister smile. He threw a right hook at me. I ducked out of the way. I went for a quick left cross, but he easily dodged me.

"You're slow, ol' man," he said contemptuously. He connected hard to my right shoulder, causing spears of pain to race through me. I feigned a right jab and landed a left cross square on his jaw. One of his teeth went flying. He retaliated with a punch to my stomach. I gave him a solid uppercut to his chin, making him stagger back as bloodshot from his mouth. Larry spit on the ground, wiping his mouth.

Larry screamed as he swung a hard right punch to my head. I blocked my face with my arms. He kneed me in the stomach before hitting me multiple times in the back. I fell on the ground hard, and my eyesight blurred. For a brief second, I saw two Larrys. All of a sudden, it felt as if time was in slow motion. Mallory's image came into my head. I could hear her calling me.

"Dad! No!"

"Mallory?" I called out to her. Larry looked at me as I did.

"What the—?" he said, confused. "What the hell's wrong with you? You have lost it, haven't you, John?"

"Dad, get up! Get up!" I heard Mallory shriek.

My head ached, my shoulder still throbbing.

"GET UP NOW!" Her voice rocked my ears.

Larry was speaking to me, but all I could hear were low garbled noises coming from his mouth. My vision and hearing returned to normal. My mind told me that my body was sore, but for some reason, I could no longer sense the pain. I was finally able to stand.

"I've never met an ox that hit like a girl before," I said.

"You do wanna die, don't you?" he retorted.

His eyes bulged; his face completely red as he rushed at me. I squatted slightly and used his momentum to help lift him straight up over my head.

I threw him and he tumbled back onto the grass. He was almost to his feet again when I slammed my fist right between his eyes. I heard his nose break. He toppled over again. I sat on top of him and grabbed his throat, squeezing as hard as I could while I bashed his head onto the ground.

"You goddamn son of a bitch! I'll fuckin' kill ya! Kill ya! Kill ya!"

All the years of friendship had meant nothing to him, and the rage I felt was unleashed. I was still slamming his head on the grass when I realized he had stopped moving. What had I done? Did I kill him? No. He was still breathing.

I dragged his body back to the nearest tree I could find, and by the time I had done so I was dead on my feet. The tree was tall and thick, just wide enough to wrap his arms behind his back and handcuff him. I searched inside his pocket and found his cell phone. I ran back and found Larry's gun where I had thrown it, putting it back in my holster. His cell phone had a signal, but it was weak. I had no idea what police district I was in.

I dialed 911.

"Emergency," a male operator answered.

"Connect me to the police, please!" I replied.

"Please state your name and location."

"Detective Sandes with the Seattle PD. I'm not sure of my location. This is urgent."

"One moment."

"District seven," a man answered.

Chapter 18

I had just finished telling everything to the police. Since I couldn't give them a specific location, they had to trace my call. I was told to stay put and wait for the police units to arrive. But I couldn't just stay there, not while Carrie and Crystal were in the hands of those maniacs. I remembered Larry pointing to the cabin earlier and remembered the general direction Locke or Marlboro Man had taken the girls. I wondered how far it could be. I picked up Larry's keys and found my way back to his car. I drove slowly, keeping my lights off so I wouldn't draw attention to myself in case Frank and Marlboro Man were lurking somewhere. About ten minutes later, I saw a cabin in the distance. I parked and exited the car about three hundred yards away, shutting the door quietly.

I could see lights on inside the house. It was hard to make anything out, but I thought I could see Frank through one of the windows. There was no sign of Marlboro Man. Maybe he was in another part of the house. There was no way I could take them both on. As I approached, I saw Frank sitting with his back to the window. I had Larry's gun. It was still dark outside, so I was pretty sure they couldn't see me. I slowly crept toward the cabin until I was just fifty yards away. I stopped to pull out the gun and then ran toward the door. I pounded loudly with my fist. I quickly stepped to the side, out of sight, and a moment later, when Frank opened the door, I grabbed his head and smashed it against the wall.

As he fell to the ground, I looked inside the cabin. Suddenly, Locke appeared toward the back of the cabin, shotgun firing.

Boom!

He almost took my head off. I didn't want to fire back inside the house since I had no idea where Carrie and Crystal were. I ran to the side of the house out of harm's way. As I peeked around the corner toward the front door, I saw Locke.

"Here, kitty, kitty. Come out and play," Locke said, smiling. He was looking around for me in the opposite direction. I aimed my gun at him, preparing to fire when he suddenly wheeled around and fired right at me.

A whole chunk of wood right next to my head exploded off the corner of the cabin. Another near hit. I fired two shots back at him, not even bothering to aim properly. I heard him reloading. I jerked around the corner again and fired, but heard only a loud snap from my gun. Shit! Out of bullets. Larry didn't even have a full magazine in this damn thing. By now Locke had finished reloading. I quickly retreated just before he had a chance to fire again. *Boom!* I heard another piece of the cabin explode behind me.

I ran behind the cabin, figuring I could sneak up behind him. Wait. No, he would expect that. I ran to the other side, peering around both corners. I didn't see any sign of him. Shit. Where the hell was he? I decided to run back the way I had come, knowing that I had a fifty-fifty chance of walking into his double-barreled shotgun. Looking around the corner again, I saw him, his back to me, creeping to the opposite side. He had to be at least six foot five, an advantage of more than half a foot over me.

Here goes nothing. I crept up behind him and jerked his shotgun away, but he kicked me in the face and knocked me off balance. The gun flew in the air. I saw him hovering over me. The shotgun lay next to me. I grabbed it by the barrel and nailed him hard in the stomach with the butt. He fell over.

We were both back up quickly. I swung the shotgun at him again, and he grabbed it by the handle. We had a tug of war for a brief moment, then he quickly let go while I fell and hit the earth. I couldn't believe I fell for that one.

I lunged for him, grabbing him around his waist. I tried to pick him up with no luck. Locke was fairly stout, probably the same weight as Larry, but much taller with a longer frame. He wrapped his arm around me, putting me into a headlock, and threw me back to the ground like a rag doll. He stood over me, and I landed a hard kick to his shin.

"Fuck!" he screamed. His other foot slammed into my stomach. He pressed harder, and the air went out of me. I had both hands wrapped around his foot. I couldn't shake him off. He was still pressing down hard on my stomach when I heard police sirens from a distance. I saw Locke look off in their direction. I gave his ankle a good twist to throw him off balance, and he staggered off me. I got up only to take a hard punch right to my forehead. I felt myself fall backward....

Chapter 19

I woke up to find several faces staring down at me, lights flashing behind them like blue haloes. It took me a moment to get my bearings. Once my eyes adjusted, I recognized the familiar uniforms.

"Are you all right, sir?" one of the officers asked me as he helped me sit up.

"Where is he? Marlboro Man. I mean Locke. Where is he?" I had to find him. I looking around frantically and tried to stand, but quickly fell back down.

"Whoa, there. Calm down sir," he said. "Are you Detective John Sandes?"

"Yes," I answered. "We need to save the girls."

"Don't worry. They're both here. We found them inside the cabin. They've already filled us in a little on what happened."

I looked past him and saw Carrie and Crystal beside each other close to a few other officers, looking tired and traumatized.

"What about the others? Did you find them?" I asked apprehensively.

"We found the Seattle police chief, Larry Wegmueller, handcuffed to a tree a few miles down the road. That's where we traced your phone call. We searched around for you too, but then we heard gunshots coming from here. We drove until we spotted this cabin and found you lying on the ground," the officer explained.

"You caught Locke, right? Marlboro Man?"

"I don't know who that is unless you're referring to this guy over here," he said, pointing to one of the patrol cars where Frank was standing with his hands cuffed behind his back. Larry was next to him. They were both surrounded by officers.

"No, there was another one."

"We didn't find anyone else."

August 3, 11:45 a.m.

The local police took us all to their station for questioning, and they talked with me most of the night. It was arranged that Carrie and Crystal would stay the night in a room at the station. If it wasn't for the girls' statements to back me up, I don't believe I would have had much of a case against Larry. Even though those officers were not from the Seattle district and didn't know Larry personally, they knew his reputation. When I arrived back in Seattle, I headed downtown to talk with the rest of the department. As I walked to my office, I drew stares from the staff. The whole city knew about what had happened. Somehow the information concerning Larry's arrest had already leaked to the press, and it was all over the news. Everyone was shocked at what Larry had done. They had no idea about these operations he was overseeing.

Penny quickly rushed over to me.

"Hello, Detective Sandes. Would you like some coffee or anything?"

"No, Penny. Thanks anyway." I could feel her worried eyes following me. As I was about to shut the door, she came into my office.

"Uh, sir, I just wanted to tell you that I think that you were very brave in what you did and… and that the rest of staff and I are proud of you."

"Thank you, Penny. I only did what should have been done."

She nodded and went back to her desk.

My desk phone rang. It was Parker. He apologized for intruding but said he was so shocked by the news that he had to ask me about it. Normally I wouldn't have said anything, but since he had helped provide me with such important information regarding the case, I gave him a brief account of the events, purposely leaving out some of the more critical details. Technically, I couldn't reveal too much information just yet. Not until after I testified. I would have many court cases and legal proceedings to attend soon. Larry was going to do whatever he could to con his way out of this, and I had to make sure justice was served. I had registered both Carrie and Crystal with a foster home. Hopefully, they would get into a good home and find some peace, once and for all.

Chapter 20

December 11, 12:00 noon

The last several months had been hell. Carrie, Crystal, and I provided statements for just about every law enforcement agency in the state. We were at the court trial, testifying against Larry, Frank, and Erotica Fliks. It's been extremely difficult for the girls. They have been through a lot. They had to describe in detail all the horrible sexual experiences they were forced to endure. They'd both cried many times during the past months, especially today. The judge just called an hour recess before the trial would resume again. For now, the girls had done everything needed, and their part was completed. They were both required to stay until the end of the trial in case their testimony was needed again. During recess, I walked outside with them.

The three of us sat on one of the concrete steps in front of the courthouse.

"Mr. Sandes, what do we do if Mr. Simone doesn't go to jail or he sends someone after us?" Carrie said worriedly.

I placed my hands on her shoulders and said, "Don't worry about anything, okay? You and Crystal will be perfectly safe. I won't let anyone harm either one of you, I promise."

Carrie looked up at me and started crying, "I'm sorry. I'm just so scared now." She hugged me tightly and I wrapped my arms around her. I could see Crystal was troubled also and pulled her in as well.

"Trust me. Everything will be alright," I said to them confidently. The three of us shared our moment.

I looked at my watch and saw it was 12:55. I knew neither of the girls wanted to go back into the courtroom.

"Carrie, Crystal, we have to go back now. Don't worry, we'll walk in side by side." I took each of them by the hand, walking back toward the courthouse entrance. We walked slowly and steadily. As we proceeded through the hallway we stopped. I looked the girls in the eyes and nodded to both of them. Everyone else was already in the courtroom. The three of us walked in together, the rest of the crowd staring at us as we prepared to await the outcome.

Epilogue

December 25

It's a cool, windy afternoon on Pacific Beach. The sun isn't shining, but it's not raining either. I am taking a long, relaxing stroll. It's fairly isolated here. A few joggers running in the distance; a woman walks her dog even farther away. Frank Simone is serving a life sentence in prison. Larry is locked up too, hopefully for many years to come. But he was able to swing some sort of deal with the district attorney's office by confessing as well as exchanging information leading to the conviction of some of the other men involved in Erotica Fliks' operation. Who knows how long he will be behind bars. Not long after Larry's arrest, Phillip Rodriguez's body was found in Elliott Bay, about 50 miles north of Duwamish Head. Lauren was a mess when I came by to inform her of the news. That was always the worst part of the job, telling someone that a loved one had passed.

I had received letters from Crystal and Carrie and learned that both of them had been adopted by a loving couple, and they were being treated very well. From what the letter said, they were like sisters now and got along wonderfully.

As I strolled, I was suddenly reminded of a dream that I had last night. I dreamed about a young married couple at their home with their two Australian shepherds. One of the dogs was constantly circling the dining room table. The other was in the living room staring into a corner, barking at the wall. The man was seated at his computer. An orange cat suddenly jumped onto the keyboard.

"Simon, get down," he said, as he grabbed the cat and tossed it gently off the desk. When the cat persisted, he put the animal outside the room and closed the door. He heard the cat scratching, trying to get in.

"Haha. Can't get in now, can ya, ya little bastard," he said playfully.

Then the dream shifted back to the barking dog. The animal was looking intently at a white pit bull in the corner. The pit bull had a light blue glow surrounding him. A woman in the same room was holding her newborn. She seemed not to notice the pit bull. Though the other dog was barking loudly, she paid no attention. She was tired but happy. She caressed her baby girl's head and smiled.

I have no idea what the dream meant. Perhaps it was my subconscious, showing me a life similar to the one I once had. Or perhaps it was about the baby. Thousands of murders occur every year in our country. The only way that I can try to find comfort is to remind myself that at least new lives are born into our world every day.

It's been more than two months since I retired. The world is changing. It's becoming stranger and more brutal every moment. Things I never thought I would see in my lifetime are happening. With all the crime and terrorism, mankind itself will inevitably destroy our planet.

I picked up the newspaper this morning and read about a young medical student who was found dead in her boyfriend's apartment. She had been shot through the heart. Her boyfriend happened to be a police officer. It smelled fishy. Her name was Holly Lane. She was twenty-eight, and she had her whole life ahead of her. Now, she would never experience marriage, the joy of having a child, or any of the other happy events that life has in store. I can only hope that her killer will be brought to justice. With all the corruption in this world, however, will anyone ever find out what happened to Holly Lane?

Emerson Locke, Marlboro Man, is still out there. They found his footprints at the scene, but so far there have been no leads as to where he may have gone. There was also no record of his past, employment, or anything. No address, phone number, or social security number. Nothing. It makes my skin crawl just thinking about him. There's nothing else I can do. My life as a detective is over. I have nothing more to give. I must be content to live with the knowledge that I did everything in my power during my career. I am finally prepared to concentrate on something else. I am ready to do other things more beneficial for my lifestyle. I hope to find Mallory, to see her again someday. I know she's out there somewhere, and I hope she realizes that I love her. I'm sorry we've been apart for so long. I accept responsibility for that and will keep searching for her.

I continued walking on the sandy beach, looking ahead.

The End